BLOOD WORSHIP

ISBN 1-59113-349-1

Published by Barbara A Mack USA.

PRINTED IN THE UNITED STATES OF AMERICA

Booklocker.com, Inc.
2003

BLOOD WORSHIP

Barbara A. Mack

For Colton and Klanci

PROLOGUE

This place was wonderful. He could not for the life of him (and he chuckled here at his own small joke) understand why he had never come here before. There were endless opportunities for taking money from the unsuspecting. And there were so many, many opportunities for feeding. He loved going downtown at night and roaming among them all. All were here to have a good time, and they drank freely of alcohol and partook surreptitiously of drugs. There was such a mix of people in the crowds, it was positively delightful, and all of them were exposing large amounts of their delectable, warm skin. They all glowed with the warmth of the blood that coursed through their veins and his eyes followed them with appreciation and hunger.

There were ripe young women with brown skin, dark hair, and limpid eyes. Others had light hair and skin almost the color of his own. Purple haired tattooed teenagers rubbed elbows with investment bankers. There were young men with old women. Old women with young men. Men with men. Women with women. All nearly naked, all happy and laughing and trusting. It was a vast cornucopia of adventure that waited for him here, in the nightlife of this Florida coastal town.

He was so handsome; all who passed him turned to stare at his silver blond hair and his ice blue eyes. Or perhaps it was his fine physique and his smooth pale skin, or the way he was dressed all in black silk. The man who called himself Sang Adorer shrugged. Who knew, or even cared why? He was attractive to humans, almost too attractive and always had been. Sometimes he would gaze back at the fascinated one who ogled him. And the one who stared would flush both with sexual excitement and fear. He amused himself by imagining the furor if he revealed himself as he really was, revealed both his hunger and his power to the crowd. They wouldn't be happy and laughing then, oh, no, they wouldn't. They would cringe before him, pay him homage, as they should. As they should.

He felt a rush of exhilaration. The changes he had seen here were amazing. What a world. This time he wouldn't make any mistakes. There would be no troubles as there had been the time before. He was aware that he had often overstepped his boundaries and grown careless because of his belief in himself and the power that he held. But not this time. He had learned something from the errors that he had made. He would build a following, guard his strength, let them do all the work. He would keep himself hidden . . . until it was time to be seen. He must be careful and lie low. He would be wary and take things slowly, until he got a firm grasp on the way of this world.

He heard a thumping, driving beat that sounded remarkably like a large heart beating and followed it around the corner. It was coming from a crowded bar with the words Scarlet Heaven emblazoned across the front in red letters. He stopped abruptly in the doorway and watched the stage where a man lapped eagerly at the thin stream of blood flowing down the neck of a woman tied in a chair. She was screaming theatrically, and the crowd was roaring.

"Hey, if it ain't your kinda place, buddy, move on," said a cranky voice behind him. "Quit blocking the door and let the rest of the freaks in."

He turned and saw a young man dressed all in leather behind him. He smiled, tenderly, sweetly, his eyes boring into the one who had dared to speak to him so. He watched the man's eyes dilate until he could barely see the color of the irises.

"It is my kind of place," he said gently as the young man took a step back, his eyes locked onto the strange pale blue ones, obviously stunned by his magnetism. "I believe that it is *exactly* my kind of place."

CHAPTER ONE

Kevin Davis finished shoving his things into his battered backpack and zipped up the top. He felt defeated as he looked at it, lying there on the bed. It sure didn't seem like much to take along. Two changes of clothing and some snacks he'd filched from the kitchen. Oh, well. He had his babysitting money, the stash that he'd hidden in his room. Oh, not the stash that Alan had found right away, but the other one. He laughed humorlessly. Alan was such an idiot, he never realized that the first one was just a decoy. Kevin had been planning this for a while, and he was *way* smarter than that ignorant Florida cracker could ever be.

He started out purposefully for the bus station, swinging his arms jauntily, trying to pretend that he was happy about it. He was really doing it. He was really running away. This wasn't some capricious decision that he'd made because he was angry. He wasn't trying to punish his mom. He wasn't into drugs. This wasn't even because he was gay.

This was because he didn't want to be raped by his mother's boyfriend, Alan.

Alan had been dating his mother for about six months. At first, he'd ignored Kevin, which was fine because he couldn't stand the man. God, how could his mother sleep with this guy? Kevin wrinkled his nose. The man *greased* his hair back like some fifties hood. He was skinny, except for the potbelly on him, and though he couldn't be more than 35, he had *absolutely* no muscle tone and his skin sagged off of him like some old lady's. He also worked as little as possible, and hadn't had a job for at least half of the time she'd been dating him. He knew that his mother was scared of being alone, but *Jesus!*

And aggravating as that all was, it had been just an annoyance until two months ago, when he'd moved in with them. Then he'd started paying a lot of attention to Kevin. A lot. But only when his mother wasn't around, and not the kind of attention that Kevin appreciated. He'd felt him watching, seen him staring when he didn't think that anyone else had noticed. He'd even tried to come into the bathroom a couple of times when Kevin was taking a shower, but he wasn't stupid and he always locked the door. And he'd started shoving a chair underneath the door handle as an extra precaution.

Alan always acted like he hated him, too, slapping him around every chance he got. Touching, he was always touching Kevin, but in some hurtful way. He made sure that it never went so far that Kevin had marks, but he knew what was coming.

Kevin knew that his mother had told Alan that he was gay. And it had taken Kevin a while, but he had finally figured the whole thing out. He wrinkled his nose. It was sick. Alan was sick. People said that *he* was unnatural, but Alan was the deviant, not him.

Alan wanted him, and he was angry about it. He wanted to have sex with him, and he wanted to hurt him when he did it.

He would catch him alone some time soon, and it would start the way that those kinds of things always did, with Alan slapping him around. Then ol' Alan would finally screw up his courage–Kevin laughed grimly to himself, that was a good one, screw up his courage—and he would do what he'd been wanting to do all along. He'd rape him and he'd hurt him, leave him bleeding on the floor, and he'd act like it was all Kevin's fault. Because he didn't want to admit that he really wanted to fuck young boys. That would make him a *fag*, and he was too macho to be a fag.

And nobody would believe that Kevin hadn't wanted it, and Alan would only get a slap on the wrist. Or maybe they wouldn't believe Kevin at all, maybe they'd think that *he'd* seduced Alan and then tried to cry rape. Because since he was fourteen years old Kevin had made it very clear exactly in which direction his sexual interests lay. Everybody in town knew it. It had been a matter of pride, for Kevin. He wasn't going to pretend to be something that he wasn't.

It might be the 21st century, but people still had the same prejudices they'd had in the previous ones. And he'd come in for his share of hazing, even from people he'd thought would understand. So he knew that there was no use talking to anybody about it. He'd tried to say something to his Mom about it, but she'd brushed it off and acted like she didn't understand what he meant. But Kevin knew that she just didn't want to understand.

As he got on the bus, Kevin tried not to think about how much he'd miss his mother.

* * *

Ah, good, at last he approaches our young friend, the old one thought hungrily. He watched avidly, a bright red tongue flicking at the lush contours of his lips. Closer, my child, closer. He took a deep breath, drawing the boy's scent deeply into his nostrils, filling himself with the smell of his prey, but careful to remain hidden in the shadows. He was too hungry to go nearer. He didn't want to scare their victim off, did he? This one had been tough to find as it was, and no doubt he would run screaming if he caught just a glimpse of what stared so ravenously at him from the shadows.

His eyes burned avidly, and he almost flew from his hiding place. He had left it too long, too long, and he must not do this again. The hunger was almost uncontrollable. He must feed more often, or he would turn on his own followers and drink them dry. And then he would have start all over again, searching for those who had the special skills he needed. And that would take too much time, it would be a waste of his energies. He would just feed more often.

The boy was nervous but tried not to act as if he were. He was pale, too, and looked unwashed. No doubt all he owned in the world was contained in that crumpled backpack he clutched.

Be quick, Dan, my trusted one, the hunter whispered, and he knew that Dan heard him when he saw him stiffen. Dan leaned forward and whispered something in the boy's ear. He placed a hand on the runaway's shoulder, who didn't flinch away, seeming instead to lean into the other man. Dan had mentioned money of course, because money was what they all wanted, these absurd children. The paper that would buy them things, dull their pain, fix their lives. But money would not change this one's life, because it would be over as soon as he agreed to Dan's proposition. He just would not know it. Yet.

The boy nodded. He was foolish and too trusting, and that worked to their advantage. He would soon grow to regret his credulousness.

He would wait for them in the house, and the boy would not be frightened at first. Then when he sees me among my followers and realizes our purpose, his terror will rise.

He smiled. The terror was so luscious. It was hard to say which he liked best, their fear or their blood.

* * *

Jessie Hartwell was dreaming when Mrs. Davis knocked on her bedroom door to tell her that a police officer was on the phone and wanted to talk to her.

"I always liked that name, Kira," Mom was saying. ***"It always made me think of the sound a hawk makes when it's flying. Kira. It's a real strong name, don't you think?"***

Jessie looked over her shoulder to see Mom curled up on that raggedy old couch she refused to get rid of.

"It's too comfortable to throw out," she always protested. ***"I've got it broke in just the way I like it."***

And Jessie always laughed when she said it, because the last three words always came out 'Ah lahk ee-it'. Mom always said she could control her accent unless she was drunk, tired, or full of strong emotion—and she was full of strong emotion all the time, so she could never really control it. It slipped out whenever it wanted to.

"She wasn't strong enough, though, baby. That name couldn't help her out of the place she got into," Mom said, and she sounded as if she'd come straight from Alabama yesterday, instead of the twenty years ago it had been.

"Something bad's happened, baby. Really bad. You got to be fearless, 'cause it's going to be hard. Scary things gonna happen. Bloody things."

And while Jessie watched, horrified, the ratty old couch began to fill up with blood. It ran in a red river over her mother's lap, who didn't seem to notice. Jessie could smell it, the blood, that awful, metallic odor filling the room. It oozed past her mother's waist and she lifted a hand now dripping with it to wave at her. Jessie watched in revulsion as the droplets went flinging across the room to land on the floor in front of her, glistening and somehow malevolent. The blood wanted her, and it trickled sluggishly toward her, joining with the other drops to form a larger mass, trying to reach her ...

"Momma," Jessie said, though she'd stopped calling her that years ago. "Momma!"

"I got to go now. Remember what I said, baby," she said intently, the blood almost to her chin. ***"It's real important."***

"Jessie, are you awake?" Mrs. Davis said, knocking a little harder on the door, really rattling it this time. She knew Jessie was hard to wake in the mornings. "There's a police officer named Bennett on the phone who wants to talk to you."

The minute Jessie opened her eyes she knew that Kira Matthews was dead.

* * *

Mrs. Davis put a hand to Jessie's cheek, where it trembled noticeably. Jessie pulled her hand down and held it tightly in her lap. Mrs. Davis wasn't holding up too good, Jessie thought. Ordinarily, her plain, good-natured face had its own kind of serene beauty, and a natural neatness helped. But stress had left its toll today and she looked like the seventy-year-old woman that she was, and a homely one at that. Her round little cheeks were sagging, her graying hair was going every which way, and the straps of her slip were showing though the top of her dress. Not how she would normally appear in public. Jessie hadn't wanted her to come to the police station with her, but Mrs. Davis had insisted, and Jessie had given in.

"It's all right," she said in reassurance. "They just want to talk to me about Kira. I'll be okay, Mrs. Davis."

"It's too much, too much," the little old lady murmured. Her hand in Jessie's felt cold, even though the air conditioning in the police station definitely wasn't keeping up its workload. It was in the high 90's outside and the humidity was nearly 90%. South Florida was always hot, even in the wintertime.

"Maybe you should talk to a lawyer first," Mrs. Davis said. "That poor girl. What was she doing down on the beach in the middle of the night? How could this have happened?"

"I guess that's what Sergeant Bennett wants to find out."

"Why's he calling you down here so early? I told him on the telephone that you'd been home all night with me, but he insisted on you coming down here this morning."

"He probably has to interview all of Kira's friends, Mrs. Davis," Jessie said. "I don't need a lawyer for that." She squeezed her hand gently. "You'll be with me, and if you think I need to get a lawyer anytime during the interview, we'll stop and get one. OK?"

The little woman was mollified. "All right, Jessie. I just don't want you getting upset. It's only been six months ..."

"I'll be OK," Jessie said, cutting her off. She didn't want to think about that right now. "You'll be with me."

She was glad when a tired forty-ish man dressed in rumpled clothing came out of an office and called her name. She didn't want to continue this conversation.

She helped Mrs. Davis to her feet, biting her lip when she realized how much the older woman was leaning on her. Mrs. Davis was in her seventies, and this was hard on her. She had known Jessie for six years, ever since Mrs. Davis had fallen and broken her ankle on her dew-dampened sidewalk one morning and Mandy Hartwell had been her home health nurse. On Saturdays, Jessie had always come with her mother to check on the spry little old lady, and the two had taken an immediate liking to each other.

When her mother had died, Mrs. Davis had insisted to Jessie that she wanted Jessie to move in with her. Eventually, she said, they would locate Jessie's aunt and then Jessie might want to stay with her. But until then, she had this huge house with all these rooms, and she lived by herself. And it certainly wouldn't be a financial burden, and Jessie could finish out her senior year of college without having to worry. And then they'd worry about next year when it got here. She'd appreciate some company, and it would be good for Jessie to stay with someone that she knew.

It had worked out well for Jessie. But it didn't seem to working quite as well for Mrs. Davis. She'd dropped at least five pounds in the last three months, and she seemed to Jessie to be shrinking even further in the last week or two. And since she barely topped 100 pounds, any weight that she lost was weight that she couldn't afford to lose. She certainly was having a lot more trouble getting around these days.

Jessie had started doing the shopping and all the cleaning at the house, just to take the burden off of her, though the old woman protested. Mrs. Davis was becoming more fragile by the day, and Jessie was afraid that she was making herself ill by taking care of her. She owed Mrs. Davis a lot. For someone who hadn't been around many young people for at least thirty years, she was surprisingly tolerant. She didn't mind that Jessie dressed Gothic on the weekends; the older woman actually seemed to enjoy Jessie's theatrical black makeup and costumes. Sometimes she'd give her suggestions on what to wear. Jessie had a black-and-red patterned scarf at home that Mrs. Davis had given her. She'd said that it had been just hanging around in her closet for years and it certainly went well with Jessie's black vinyl bustier and short skirt, so she might as well keep it. Jessie wore it all the time, and it made her feel good that Mrs. Davis knew that you couldn't tell what a person was like by looking at the clothes that they wore. Not everybody was like that, and Jessie came across a lot of prejudice.

Sergeant John Bennett looked sternly at Jessie, and she guessed that was his most frequent expression, because his forehead fell immediately into little furrows. She also guessed that he was not quite as liberal as Mrs. Davis was. He looked at her sitting there in her black clothing, wearing the silver-studded dog-collar bracelet and necklace, and he didn't sneer, exactly, but Jessie could tell that he wanted to.

"When did you last see Kira Matthews?" he asked, after establishing that the two girls had known one another since they were very young, attended the same college and frequently spent time together. He wrote everything she said down in a little notebook that lay on his desk.

"On Friday, at school," Jessie said. "I told you that already."

Sergeant Bennett turned a page in the notebook, read something, and frowned more deeply. He leaned on his elbows on the desk and stared intently at her.

"I understand that your mother, Amanda Hartwell, was killed a few months ago," he said sharply.

Jessie heard Mrs. Davis suck in a breath.

"Yes," was all she said. She trembled, inside, but refused to let him see it. *I don't want to talk about it, I don't want to talk about it!*

"And that crime hasn't been solved," he said. "I read the whole file, Jessie. Your mother's car wouldn't start, so she told her co-workers that she was going to take the bus home. They offered to give her a ride, but they had dinner reservations and she knew it, so she refused. They saw her walk down to the bus stop and sit on the bench, and then they drove off. Two fishermen found her body three days later in a canal." He consulted the notebook on his desk again. "You have an aunt somewhere, but she's traveling in Europe and no one has been able to contact her so far. No other close relatives, is that right?"

"That's right," was all that Jessie answered, though she trembled inside.

At least he didn't mention that when they called my father, he hung up on them. And my grandfather did the same thing. Neither of them even came to the funeral, and they sure never bothered to find out if I was okay, Jessie thought. *Mom always said that we had each other but now she's dead. I'm sure this asshole cop knows all that, and at least he left that part out, but I don't like him any better for it. He's playing with me, so let him work for it, I'm not going to help him torment me. If he's got something to say, let him say it.*

But she still wasn't ready when he went in for the kill.

"What would you say if I told you that your friend Kira was killed in exactly the same manner as your mother was? She was stabbed and beaten. There are more than fifty stab marks on her body; she was slashed to bits. Most of her blood drained out during the killing. It was savage. Brutal. Maybe it's even intended to send a message." Sergeant Bennett stared at her suddenly white face and ignored a twinge of conscience.

"Some of Kira's friends told me that she was into the Goth lifestyle, and it looks as if you are, too. Was Kira doing drugs? How about your mother? Because I've got to tell you that it seems very likely that this is connected to the drug traffic that runs up and down the Florida coast." He leaned back in his chair. "Especially considering that they both tested positive for methamphetamines. And it seems awfully funny to me that two people so close to you have died in exactly the same manner. Almost makes me think you might know more about this than you're saying. Are you involved, Jessie? Maybe your mother had a boyfriend in the drug business. Maybe you're in the drug business. Maybe Kira was. I don't know. All I know is that I think that you should speak up now with anything that you know before more of your friends and family are butchered."

"How dare you?" Mrs. Davis said quietly while Jessie shook in her chair. "How dare you say such a thing to this innocent young girl? She is still in *mourning*, and then this terrible incident happens, and you dare to imply that she is involved? That she is somehow peripherally responsible for the deaths of both her mother and her friend? That because she chooses to dress in a way that you don't approve of, she must be on drugs? You cannot make accurate judgements of others based on their manner of dress, Sergeant, and you should know that by now. I plan to make a formal complaint against you, young man."

"I'm here to do my job, not win a popularity contest," the big man said, but his face reddened with the criticism.

"Do it some other way," Mrs. Davis said crisply and pulled Jessie to her feet. "That was the end of cooperation from both of us. There will be no more questions and no more answers. We are leaving, and I can only hope that you have enough human feeling left in you to make you sleep badly tonight. God knows that this poor girl probably will. Good day. Come, Jessie."

He jumped at the sudden *swap* when she slapped her cane down onto his desk, right into the middle of all of his papers. Mrs. Davis smiled grimly, and then she swept regally out the door, pulling Jessie with her. Jessie noticed that the little old woman showed no signs of weakness now.

* * *

Ten blocks away, Dan Jackson was lying on his lumpy bed thinking about the night before. He smiled dreamily and licked his lips. It just kept getting better and better. But he had to figure out some way to speed up the process of getting to know these poor dumb kids. Some of them took weeks to lure in.

Who knew that drinking blood could be so much fun?

Ironically, Dan inspired trust in all who saw him. As a child, his was the face of the kid brother on television shows, the too-cute kid that could never do anything wrong. His cheeks were plump and scattered with freckles, he had a snub nose, and his hair was always cut too short on top, making it stick up endearingly. His small mouth smiled a lot, and his eyes crinkled merrily when he did so. He looked kind, and guileless, and you wouldn't hesitate to invite him right on into your house if he showed up on your doorstep. He was every-man; average height, average weight, average looks. He was the man who held doors open for little old ladies, the kind of guy that would stop to help you change your tire even if he was late for work, the one who handed back the extra twenty at the bank when they gave him too much change.

Even the people he helped to murder couldn't believe it until the very second that he struck home the knife. Not Dan. Not good old Danny-boy.

He was twenty-four, but looked younger. He still lived with his grandmother in the shabby apartment that had been his home since the age of twelve. That was the year his parents had died in a car accident, coming back from Fort Myers Beach after a long day of fun and sun. Dan had only received minor injuries.

In the months to come, he'd often wished that he'd died with them. His embittered grandmother talked incessantly of all the bad things that had happened in her life, not the least of which was having a puny little crybaby foisted off on her. That son of hers had been bad enough, the ungrateful bastard, running off like that with that slut and leaving her to struggle all alone. But his kid . . . If she didn't have such a strong sense of duty, why, she'd have just put him in foster care. But the good Lord knew that she'd never shirked her responsibilities. She'd make a man out of him, and he could never forget how much he owed her. No, he owed all he would become to dear old Granny.

Ten days after his 13th birthday he was sent to a juvenile detention center for the first of ten times. And those were only the times that they caught him. He went away most often for burglary and vandalism, and violence was always mixed in there somewhere, always a part of the crime. His rage always bubbled to the top.

At twenty-one he spent six months in a psychiatric facility after police caught him masturbating outside the window of the teenage girl he'd been stalking. He'd been warned to stay away from her several times. That was his wake up call. Not that he'd stopped. He just stopped getting caught. He never wanted to go back to jail again.

Yeah, he owed it all to dear old Granny.

But stalking wasn't enough for him anymore since he'd met Sang Adorer. Just watching them in their perfect homes with their perfect parents and fantasizing about being part of their perfect lives was not nearly enough. Now, he wanted their blood, too. He wanted to watch them die shrieking in pain. He wanted to lick their blood from his lips as they screamed in agony and he wanted to lick it from the lips of the others.

The first time that he'd killed someone had been hard for him, and he didn't like it much. As a matter of fact, he'd retched for hours afterwards, and the image of the dead woman had tormented him for days. But it grew on him, murder did. The meth helped, and Dan took a lot of it. Now he craved it, both the drugs and the murder, wanted to do it more and more and more. He smiled mistily to himself. Mere months ago, he'd felt so bored that he'd wanted to die. Now, he felt as if he were at an eternal party.

And the party was just getting started.

* * *

"I can't believe it," Shannon wailed. "I just can't believe it."

Jessie had called her friend with the hope that talking to her would make her feel better. But so far it wasn't working.

"Shannon, there's more. I forgot to tell that cop, that Bennett guy, because he freaked me out so bad. But Kira told me that she was going to some Goth party Friday night. She asked me to go along, but I said no, because I was feeling kind of sick after lunch. Kira knew that I liked to get dressed up all Gothic with her and go out, just to watch the so-called normal people stare. Do you know anything about a party that Friday? Did she ask you to go with her?"

"Oh my god! No, I didn't hear about any Goth party, or I'd have been there. That just sent a shiver down my spine. You were too sick to go, and I didn't hear about it . . . We could both be dead, too, you know."

"I just keep thinking that if I did go, maybe Kira wouldn't be . . . maybe she wouldn't . . . "

"You can't think like that," Shannon said sharply. "You can't think if only, if only. That doesn't bring them back. You just have to go on from where you are and do what you can."

Jessie gripped the receiver so hard that her knuckles hurt. "I know," she said softly. "That's why I want to look around and see what I can find out about this party she went to."

"No!" Shannon said in a panicked voice. "That's too dangerous. You don't know what you're getting into."

"I have to," Jessie said stubbornly. "I'm just going to see what I can learn about other people that went to this party. I know a lot of people at college who are into the Goth lifestyle, and they're like you and me and Kira. We just like to dress up and look different, 'cause we think it's cool, and we know that the 'normal' people are crazier than we are. But I've been hearing about these guys that are into some really strange shit. Kira and I went to a whole bunch of these parties together, and once she told me that she'd heard something about this splinter group or something . . . that they have this blood obsession. She said that she'd heard that people were cutting each other's wrists and drinking their blood. And she said that they were heavy into meth. We were a little queasy about it, too, but not enough to stop going to parties. We didn't know anybody like that. Maybe she stumbled onto the wrong kind of party and one of them went too far or something. Because that cop, that Bennett guy, he said something about Shannon testing positive for methamphetamines."

"You're being foolish," Shannon said in a brittle voice. "Let that cop figure it out. You don't need to get into this."

"She wasn't just *killed*, Shannon," Jessie said intently. "She was high on crank, and you know she wasn't into that. She drank and she smoked a little weed once in a while, but she never did anything heavy. She told me about a million times that she was never going to end up like her brother Tom, who's in rehab like every other month. And that's not all, Shannon. Somebody mutilated her, did something terrible to her. Like they did to my Mom."

"Oh, Jessie, is that what this is all about?" Shannon asked softly. "Your Mom? That is just one more reason to leave this whole thing alone. You always idolized your mother way too much, Jessie, and you've made her up into some kind of Supreme Being in your mind now that she's dead. She wasn't perfect; she could be rude and shallow and stupid just like everybody else. Get over it; you're too old to be a mama's girl. Your mother took drugs and then somebody killed her; it happens every day, and Kira just changed her mind, she was probably in the middle of a party situation and she made a bad decision. And while she was high and vulnerable, she got hooked up with some crazy who hacked her to pieces. You can't go around trying to find out who the crazy is. He's probably long gone by now, anyway. Let the cops deal with it. Let it alone."

"I can't," Jessie said, keeping her voice steady with an effort. "I know that my mother wasn't perfect, Shannon. I know exactly what she was like. I could always see her clearly, and she was never the kind of person who could sit up on a pedestal; she was way too real for that. But she didn't mess with drugs like crank, and she didn't deserve to die. And neither did Kira. And *I* don't deserve to be talked to this way, so I want an apology."

"You're right," Shannon said. "You know I loved your mom, too. But I think you're going over the edge, Jessie, and you don't need to get involved with this. This is scary."

"I want you to ask around, Shannon," Jessie said resolutely. "I figure somebody who was at that party will have to know something about the maniac who likes to kill people and mangle their bodies. I've got to find out. Ask some of your Goth friends if they've heard anything about this. Come on, we've been friends a long time," she said as Shannon hesitated. "Do it for me, even if you think I'm being crazy."

"All right," Shannon said reluctantly. "I'll ask a few people if they've heard anything. But that's all. And you've got to promise me that you won't do anything stupid, okay? If you find something out, take it to the cops."

"All right," Jessie said. "I'll go to the cops if we find out anything," she said, but she knew that she was lying. She wasn't going to tell the cops anything; she didn't trust them. That Bennett guy was just typical of the breed. They didn't care, as long as they had somebody to pin it on, and if they could pin it on a bunch of Goth freaks, so much the better. Didn't matter to *them* if it was the right person they put away or not, but it did to her. And Jessie was going to find out who it was and they were going to pay for taking Kira away. They were all going to pay.

* * *

Rae Ann Davis began to realize soon after she left the bar with him that she had made a big, big mistake.

She'd agreed to come with him because he was so normal, usually so nice and friendly when she saw him in the bar where she worked. It wasn't like he was a stranger. He had been coming in two, three nights a week for the last year or so, and she'd always spent a little time flirting with him. All the waitresses did. He was good-looking, for one thing; he was the blond beach-boy type that she went for, *and* he was nice, and he tipped big. And all three of those things were hard to find in the same package. Rae Ann knew, because she'd been out there looking.

So when he'd asked her to go somewhere with him after work, she'd thought, why not? Why not go out with him and have a little fun? She was always working when everybody else was partying, so why shouldn't she have her turn?

But it was getting just a little too weird for her. When he'd asked her to go with him, she had thought that he meant to his house. Not hiking over the river and through the woods to some shack out in the middle of nowhere. Rae Ann drew her jacket around her arms and glared around. What was this nasty place? And what was that *smell*?

She protested to him, and he laughed and grabbed her tightly, pulling her into his body. His eyes looked manic, and Rae Ann knew that she shouldn't have come. When she told him that she wanted to go home, he only sneered.

"What's the matter?" He shook her roughly for emphasis, scaring her. "You're not talking your way out of this. I know exactly what you are. You're a whore. Did you think that you could hide it from me forever? A whore!"

He slammed her against the wall so hard that she thought her head would go through the plaster. Her back and shoulders felt bruised, and the blow stunned her.

"You're going to pay, you bitch," he said into her face. "You've been swinging your ass at me for a long time, teasing me and leading me on, and you're going to pay up now. Always walking around with your tits and your ass hanging out, flaunting them at me; now I'm going to use you like the whore that you are."

He kept shaking her, shaking her, his hands gripping her wrists cruelly and painfully. Then he began to strike her, over and over, in the face, and on the head, calling her names as he did so.

"No!" Rae Ann cried out between the blows. "I'm not like that. I came with you because I liked you. I really liked you!"

He gave her wrists a vicious twist, bringing her to her knees. He tugged her arms behind her back and tied her wrists together. Dazed and only half-conscious by now, she only dimly felt what he was doing. His hands slipped under the short skirt that she wore to work and ripped at her panties; she could hear the cloth tear.

And then he tumbled her onto her back and unbuckled his belt.

Rae Ann trembled all over and stared up at him as he put the belt around her neck and pulled it tight, wrapping the end around one hand and using the other to guide his thick shaft into her unwilling body.

As he pumped on top of her and she struggled for breath, all she could see was his face. His nice, normal handsome face had been contorted into that of a monster.

"No, Corey," she managed to croak when he loosened the belt momentarily. "Please. Please."

But he only laughed and tightened the belt again. And Rae Ann knew that she was never going to get to leave this house; she was going to die here, in this filthy place.

CHAPTER TWO

The funeral for Kira took place five days later, after the police released her body. It was the kind of perfect day when the Florida skies are deep and cloudless, and the humidity is low enough that the heat is bearable. But as Jessie stood with Mrs. Davis and Shannon in the cemetery next door to the church, she thought that the atmosphere was all wrong. It should have been cloudy and raining, she thought darkly. There should have been thunder and lightning, and wind to whip them. Not the sun shining brightly down on them all. It shouldn't be just like every other day in Florida. This day was different because Kira was dead.

David and Teresa Matthews stood gazing vacantly at the coffin that contained the remains of their only child, as if they hadn't quite figured out what had happened yet. Their son Tom and daughter Caitlin stood behind them, both of their faces swollen from their tears. Once, as Tom swayed, Mr. Matthews had to put out a hand and pull him upright. Kira's parents seemed calm throughout the ceremony, almost placid. But as the minister uttered the last words of the service and the coffin was slowly lowered into the ground, an anguished wail of sorrow suddenly welled from Teresa Matthews' throat, and she heaved herself into her husband's arms, burying her face against him. Jessie was upset by the woman's obvious pain, and she clutched Mrs. Davis' arm and looked away, her own throat feeling tight. She knew just how Teresa Matthews felt, because she'd felt exactly the same way at her mother's funeral.

Jessie kept her face turned resolutely away from the spot holding her mother's tombstone. She'd never visited her mother's grave. She couldn't see her mother's name written on that smooth stone. She wouldn't be able to bear it. Maybe some time in the future, but not now. She wanted to cry now, but she knew that once she began, she wouldn't be able to stop, and she didn't want to do that here.

Shannon didn't seem to be holding up very well, either. Her face was pale, not its normal rosy color, and she stood listlessly beside Jessie, her head down and her eyes hidden behind dark glasses. Her parents were here somewhere, too, because her mother had been a friend to Teresa Matthews since the girls had all been in grade school together, but Shannon had elected to stand with Jessie. Maybe she thought that Jessie needed some extra support, considering that the last time she had been here it had been to bury her mother in the dark, dank ground.

Jessie was surprised how many of Kira's friends from college had shown up. She didn't know that some of these kids had even known Kira. Most of them had probably never lost anyone to death before, and some looked grief stricken and were openly sobbing. Others just slouched beside each other looking shocked.

Angelique Alea waved to her, and Jessie smiled at her. She knew Angelique slightly, and she knew that Kira had hung out with her a little bit, though she said that Angelique could be just too intense for her sometimes. Jessie felt a wisp of amusement. Kira had always said that Angelique had too much energy; she made Kira tired, and she couldn't spend more than two hours in her company without having to go home and take a nap.

Andy Mossiman held onto one of Angelique's hands with both of his, and he was staring at the ground. He raised his head when Angelique said something to him, long enough to give Jessie a brief, ghastly smile. Jessie looked around at the rest of them, wondering what they were all thinking. Were they, like her, wondering if any of the others in the crowd knew what had happened to Kira? She'd tried asking around at college about the party that Kira had been going to attend that Friday night, but she'd gotten few answers. A lot of them seemed to think that she was blaming Goths for Kira's death, but that wasn't true. She just wanted to know what had happened.

She walked with Mrs. Davis toward the Matthews, and as they came close, Jessie held out her hand to Kira's mother. But Teresa would have none of that. She'd known Jessie Hartwell since the girl was in kindergarten, and she drew Jessie into her arms.

"I'm so sorry," Jessie said against her silk-covered shoulder. "I loved her so much."

Teresa's hand caressed Jessie's hair as the girl left her arms.

"She loved you, too," she said, and her faint smile faded as her eyes wandered to her daughter's grave. For a moment she seemed about to dissolve into tears again, but she struggled for control and found it as Mrs. Davis held out a palsied hand to her. Teresa turned away from Jessie, trying to force herself to smile as the older woman conveyed her sympathies.

"I gotta go," Shannon muttered suddenly in Jessie's ear, and took off without saying anything to either of Kira's parents. Jessie stared after her. Shannon was almost running out the gates of the cemetery.

* * *

Jessie was working on a project for one of her classes when the telephone began to ring. Mrs. Davis was next door visiting with her friend, and cursing under her breath, Jessie got up to get it. There was a phone on the desk in the hallway, and she couldn't stand to listen to it ringing. She picked it up on the fifth ring, right before the answering machine would pick it up.

"Hello?"

Nobody answered. But Jessie could hear breathing on the line. She huffed air from her nose impatiently. What kind of perv got a thrill from making crank phone calls? God knows what he was doing on the other end of the line. She started to hang up, and then heard her name spoken softly.

"Jessie... I can see you."

"Who is this?" she asked sharply.

"Leave this alone. Do you hear? Leave this alone unless you want to end up like Kira."

Fear slid down her spine like a drop of icy water. The voice was husky and hoarse; a disguised croak that she couldn't decipher, though she tried.

"Just leave it alone."

"Who is this? What are you talking about? Leave what alone?"

"I know where you go, and I know what you do," the voice whispered. "So leave it alone, Jessie. Or I'll know and I'll come for you."

The phone went dead, and Jessie stared at the receiver in her hand. She was afraid, and the ice that had dripped down her spine now spread over her entire body until she was shaking with the cold. She dropped the phone and dropped into a fetal position beside the wall. Someone was trying to frighten her, to keep her from asking questions about Kira's death. Otherwise, why would they mention her name?

Then a sudden scalding anger began to chase the cold from her body. Just who the hell did they think that they were dealing with here? Some scared little kid who'd back off at the first hint of danger? No, she was Mandy Hartwell's daughter, and they could go fuck themselves. They had no idea who they were dealing with; threats didn't work with her. Her mother had always said that the best way to get anyone in her family to do something was to tell them that they couldn't, and she was right.

Nobody told her what to do, especially not some psycho pervert who had to resort to crank calls to get what he wanted. She wouldn't let him win.

Jessie stood up.

She slammed the telephone back down onto the receiver and marched back down the hallway to her room. She flipped open her book and began to do her homework again. But the warmth from her fit of anger didn't last, and soon she was cold again, almost shaking. She set her mouth in a grim line and went to get a sweater.

Fuck him, whoever it was. She was cold and she was afraid, but that was okay. She wouldn't let anything stop her. She wouldn't say anything to Mrs. Davis, either. She would only worry, and what could she do about it, anyway? It was best to just keep it to herself.

* * *

Shannon woke slowly. Darkness surrounded her, yet her room was filled with a strange shimmering glow, as if the glow of the moon was somehow shining inside the room itself. It must be a full moon, she thought groggily. But when she looked out the window beside her bed, the night was a deep silken ebony. There was no moon anywhere that she could see.

The glow was in the room itself. She sat up and gasped audibly.

On her dresser sat a giant owl. She'd seen owls before, but usually they were the small burrowing owls of this area and this was a barn owl. She'd only seen these in pictures before, and she was sure that she'd never seen one this large before. As she watched, it spread its thickly feathered wings and seemed to stretch the way that she did when she woke from a nap. Shannon pulled the covers up to her neck, scrunching down into her warm bed. What was happening here?

But the owl turned its head toward her and she saw that it was not here to hurt her. The light came from its blind eyes, a cold radiance that lit up the darkness of her room. The owl's beak moved, and sound came from its throat, a high, screeching noise that was still recognizable as speech. And despite the distortion, she knew that voice. She knew it well.

"Come to me," the owl said, and Shannon covered her ears with the shrillness of it.

"Come to me."

And then it spread its wings again and the room filled with a light so bright that she covered her eyes to protect them. When she opened them again, the owl was gone. Numbly, she stood and began searching for her clothes.

She must go to him. He had called. Her master needed her.

Maria Alonzo had gone to bed early that night, worn out from the funeral. She couldn't go to another funeral, she'd thought wearily before crawling under the covers of her neatly made bed. Mandy Hartwell's funeral was bad enough, but Kira ... She wasn't much more than a child, with her whole life ahead of her. It was too much. Maria had fallen into an exhausted sleep that had more to do with the emotional roller coaster she felt she'd been on than any actual physical weariness.

But she woke up around midnight feeling that something was wrong. Something that didn't have anything to do with the events of the day. There was something wrong in the house.

She forced herself to lie still in the bed for a moment, listening to her husband snore quietly, straining to hear anything else. She could hear nothing but the normal sounds of the night, but the sense that something was wrong wouldn't leave her. She got out of bed, being careful not to wake Marco. She slipped into her bathrobe and left her room, shutting the door quietly behind her.

She turned on the hallway light and peeped into Katherine's room and smiled. The child of her middle years, her four-year-old daughter Katherine, was asleep on her back, her hair spread out on the pillow, her body spread-eagled on the bed. Katherine Alonzo slept like she lived—all over her space. She was the queen, even when she was asleep.

Maria hesitated at Shannon's door. Shannon had been so funny about her privacy lately. But something had woken her. She tapped softly. When there was no response, she opened the door and looked inside.

Shannon's bed covers were thrown back, and the room was empty. Maria hurried to the window to peer out into the night, but it was too dark, she couldn't see anything. She leaned her forehead against the cold pane of glass, closing her eyes. And when she opened them again, she thought that she saw a figure slipping into the shadows of the bushes.

"I'm going to kill that girl," she muttered to herself. "She think that she can go slipping around all hours of the night, but she will learn." She muttered a few choice words in Spanish as she belted her robe more securely and marched toward the front door. Some curses just sounded better in her native language.

"Shannon," she hissed as she stepped onto the lawn in her bare feet. "Get in here. I know you think that you're an adult, but as long as you live in this house, you will follow my rules."

She hurried around to the side of the house where she'd seen the figure, and smiled grimly when she noticed that the door to the shed was open. The girl was going to have to be smarter than that if she was going to put one over on her.

"Shannon, are you there?" she said in a low voice, her eyes searching through the darkness of the shed. She began to feel uneasy, as if eyes were watching her from the blackness. And something smelled funny in here. She'd make Marco take a look around tomorrow. It smelled like something *dead* was in the shed. She took a step back when she heard a small noise in the depths of the darkness.

"Shannon?" she called again, her voice hesitant. "Is that you?"

It was only instinct that saved her. When the sound at the back of the shed swelled into a snarl and something came charging out of the blackness at her, she jerked back and slammed the door of the shed shut. Something thudded hard against it, and Maria fled back across the yard, flew into the house and slammed the door behind her.

What had been in the shed? And where was Shannon? She was just about to go and wake her husband when she heard the back door open.

"Shannon?" she called hesitantly, her pulse jumping. And she couldn't contain her relief when her daughter stepped around the corner, her face pale.

"Where were you?" she demanded, her fear turning into anger. "Do you know what time it is? I don't mind you going out, but you must at least tell me when you're going!"

Shannon shrugged off the hand she put on her arm. Her eyes darkened with an anger of her own.

"I went for a walk," she said sullenly. "I was thinking about Kira, and about Jessie's mom. I couldn't sleep."

Maria felt her heart melt. This must be so hard for her, coming up against the realities of the world all in the space of a few months. All young people thought themselves immortal, and then to find out that they were not ... The truth that rules our lives is difficult to accept; eventually, we all must die.

Shannon had turned twenty-one some months ago, but in many ways she was still a child. Her daughter was just learning this, and Maria remembered what that felt like. And it was hard to talk to parents. She must have lain awake, thinking about it, agonizing for hours, but didn't want to bother her, didn't want to wake her mother up to talk. She still thought that being an adult meant handling everything alone, when the reverse was actually true. A true adult knew that everything is easier if it is shared. Maria felt tears sting her eyes and she hugged the girl fiercely, ignoring the stiffness of Shannon's body in her embrace.

"Go to bed, Shannon," she said gently. "It will seem better in the light of the day."

In the morning, Marco could find no trace of a dog in the shed, and Maria never thought another thing about it. It had gotten away, that was all. No big deal. She'd call animal control and have them come out and look around the neighborhood, so that the dog wouldn't try to attack anyone else.

But in the weeks to come, she kept waking up in the middle of the night, feeling a strange compulsion to check on her children, to make sure that all the windows and doors were locked. In the daytime, she dismissed her fears as silly. Marco laughed at her, and she laughed with him. She was just worrying, that was all. It was her nature.

But every time she woke up in the middle of the night, her heart pounding with the fear that she felt and her sheets soaked through with sweat, she *knew* that something was wrong. Maria was Cuban, and Cuban history was steeped in voodoo and superstition. It was hard to leave behind completely the beliefs of her childhood, and though her family liked to scoff, she knew that the 'feelings' she often got were real. She got the feeling now that something out there was watching her, and watching her family. Out there watching, and waiting. But waiting for what, she didn't know.

* * *

In the darkness, he listened to the distant sound of a dog howling plaintively and he wondered why the sound bothered him so. He knew that there must be a reason that the dog was howling. What was it? Was it howling because it knew that its own death was coming? Did death stalk someone that it loved? Or was it warning him?

Somewhere deep inside his brain, the brain now twisted up into knots with meth and crack, he knew that he was being paranoid. He had moments of lucidity; moments in which he knew that there were great holes inside his brain that the drugs had made there. He'd know, then, that he'd gone too far; and he knew that he should stop and should seek help of some kind. Then the rational moment would go away, and his thought processes would twist and turn bizarrely inside his head like dueling, hissing snakes once again.

He knew that they were trying to kill him. And that death would come in the middle of the night to get him.

He lay still beneath the snowy sheets, strips of moonlight leaking through the curtains and painting strange shapes with shifting, glowing colors on the floor. He hadn't been asleep; he hadn't slept for three days. He didn't want to go to sleep, because he was afraid. They had put a monster in his stomach, and it ate him from the inside out. It gnawed with bloody teeth and scratched with bloody talons at his intestines, growling and grunting inside of him. And if he went to sleep, it would finish him off.

The dog stopped howling, and he wondered idly if they'd killed it, too. If they'd eaten its face off and played in its blood. That was what they wanted to do to him. They wanted his blood.

He began to whimper in his bed, thrashing and turning. And he thought about going outside, the way that they wanted, the way that they whispered for him to... He could hear them. *Come outside, Corey, come and play* ...

No! he thought. No. That's what they want. I won't go outside in the darkness and the trees and the moon. Tomorrow I'll leave, I'll go far away, away from all this, and they won't be able to find me.

But he knew that he was only fooling himself. He couldn't leave. He had a house, and a job, and they would hunt him down anyway, wherever he went. And he needed the drugs that they gave him. They knew everything that he was doing and thinking anyway; they were watching his every move. He'd heard little clicks on his phone, and there had been someone peering in the window one night …

And now they'd put the monster in his belly. And the monster wanted blood. If Corey didn't feed it, it would take *his* blood. He'd thought that it would be satisfied with the girl he'd given it the other night, but it hadn't been enough for the monster. It wanted more.

Corey crawled out of bed and went to the window. He strained hard to see through the darkness, but all he saw were mutating, transforming shadows. It seemed still and quiet out there, but he knew that it was only an illusion. They were watching him.

He started to turn on the television in his room, but he knew that they watched him through the screen so he left it off. He'd found that out one day when the cable had went out; through the static he'd seen Dan's face peering at him. Since then, he'd never turned it back on.

Maybe I'll eat, he thought. He didn't think that he'd done that for a while; he kept forgetting. Corey went and rummaged through the refrigerator. There wasn't much there; eating hadn't been a priority with him lately, but he managed to find some cheese slices and bologna that didn't look too bad. He smeared mayonnaise on two slices of bread and slapped the sandwich together, stuffing almost half of it in his mouth at one bite. And he slurped down the soft drink he found in one great big gulp.

He stood staring at the back of the refrigerator while he ate. The light flickered and Corey knew suddenly what he was supposed to do. He dropped the rest of his sandwich where he stood and left the refrigerator door standing open.

He moved through the house without turning the lights on; it was strange how alien the familiar objects can look in the dark. The furniture seemed to leap forward when he turned his head; he could see it out of the corner of his eyes, but when he turned his head sharply, it all went back to where it was before. And once he became convinced that the mirror on the wall was twisting itself into a hideous monster, just waiting for him to come close enough to grab him. He stared at it until it changed itself back into a mirror again. He didn't have time for this; the light in the refrigerator had told him that he had to see something.

He turned on the television. At first it was nothing but static, but then he began to see the picture, and Corey giggled with excitement. He saw the hand holding the knife, and he knew that it was *his* hand. He saw the man standing there, saw him stagger from the inhuman force of the blow to the face, his glasses flying off of his nose to land across the room. And the knife tore through flesh and cartilage with a ripping sound, and then hacked through to the brain. The corpse sagged to the floor, blood flowing down, flowing everywhere. And Corey giggled even more when he saw that the corpse still shuddered and twitched in the throes of death.

And he knew what he had to do.

Dan had shown him. It had been Dan on the TV, just like before. But this time he hadn't been spying; he had shown Corey what to do to keep the monster from killing him, from eating his guts. He had to kill. He had to kill the man on the television.

"Okay, Dan," he said out loud, and the sound of his voice reverberated through the quiet house. "I'll do it. Thanks for showing me that."

It was going to be so easy, too. Because Corey knew that the man was an insomniac and he often went to his office at night to work. His car would be parked right out front, so it would be easy to tell if he was there. The office was isolated, and Corey could get in and out without notice.

The man trusted him, so it would be easy for Corey to get close. He stopped by the office to visit all the time when the man was working. To check on him, because that was Corey's job.

Because Corey was a cop.

Corey got high before he left; Dan had told him that the monster needed drugs, too. He was still giggling when he arrived at the building. This was going to be fun. He hoped that the monster liked it as much as he did.

* * *

Someone was following her. She had a stalker. Phoebe knew about stalkers, everybody did, but they belonged in somebody else's life. If she was a singer, or a famous actress, or even fantastically beautiful, maybe she could understand.

But she wasn't any of those things. She was just an ordinary woman with an ordinary job and an ordinary life. Phoebe looked at herself in her bathroom mirror. She was in her early twenties, dressed neatly in a business suit, with a slender figure and big blue eyes. Heads didn't turn when she walked down the street, but she had her own share of admirers.

Ordinary.

And she was beginning to wonder if it was one of the men that she'd dated who was stalking her. She didn't know; it was getting harder and harder to think. She couldn't sleep at night, and when she did drop off, her sleep was filled with nightmares. She woke every morning with an impending sense of doom.

Maybe today would be the day that he struck. And when she made it through the day, her nerves stretched tight enough to bounce quarters off of, she thought: Maybe it will be tomorrow.

This can't go on, she thought to herself. It can't. I can't take anymore.

She glanced at the slim, elegant watch on her wrist. It was time to leave for work. She looked around at her condo, where she had lived for the last year. She was proud of her house; she'd bought it with her own money, and until recently it was her haven of peace, the place where she went and was safe.

Now it felt like a prison. Because someone had been in here while she was gone, not just once but several times, and moved her things around. And she would report it to the police, but what could she say?

Officer, someone came into my house while I was at work and moved my jewelry box three inches to the right. No, they didn't take anything, just moved it. And they rifled through my underwear drawer, and I know this because I always fold up my underwear, and they were all crumpled up. Oh, and one of my least expensive perfumes is gone. Yes, that's all, just the $10 cologne that I bought at a drugstore chain. Oh, and I feel like someone's watching me all the time, at work, while I'm driving home, when I'm lying by the pool in my bikini . . . Yes, I'll be sure and call you when I get some *evidence* that someone is watching me. Thank you, Officer, for letting me make a fool of myself.

When Phoebe went outside to get into her car and go to the bank where she'd worked for five years, she stuck her head out of the front door and looked both ways before going all the way outside. Then she ran to the car, pushing the button on her clicker to unlock the doors right as she reached it. After sliding inside quickly, she locked the door with hands that trembled and headed downtown, with the sun shining brightly down on her. She felt the back of her neck crawl, and she felt near tears.

Because regardless of the lack of evidence, she knew that someone was watching her. She had an unsettled feeling, and she knew that he was behind her, following her. Was that him, there in the blue Audi? Maybe it was the guy in the silver Lexus. It could be anybody, and she felt so confused and upset.

She turned the car into the parking lot of the bank and went inside. She felt safe here, simply because there were so many people around. At nine am, the bank was buzzing with people. When Phoebe got to her desk and threw her purse down, her supervisor approached. He smiled at Phoebe, and she felt suddenly cold.

Maybe it was him.

Maybe his distinguished looks and fatherly manner hid a monstrosity. Maybe underneath his silver hair was the brain of a psychopath, and he was only waiting for the day when he could show her his secret self. The day that he would kill her.

Phoebe decided then and there that the next time she felt that someone had been in her house, she would call the police. Because if she started imagining things like this of poor Brian, it was time to get someone else to help her with this problem. Brian would probably have a heart attack and keel over if he knew what she was thinking, and a broad smile suddenly crossed her face. Brian beamed back. He was a nice man. And Phoebe felt better. Because even if the police laughed at her, at least she'd feel that she'd done something.

But Phoebe had left it too late.

When she didn't show up for work the next two days, her co-workers got uneasy and called the police. Phoebe had never missed a day's work without calling, they told the police. And they couldn't get her on the phone. When the two officers opened the door to her condo, they found something resembling a charnel house. One of the officers had been a cop in Miami for twenty years before transferring here; he boasted once that he'd seen everything, and that nothing made him sick anymore. But he joined his rookie partner in the bushes after ten seconds of seeing what someone had done to Phoebe Walker.

She didn't even look human anymore.

And that stuff congealed in the bottom of her good crystal goblets looked an awful lot like blood.

CHAPTER THREE

"Will you please hurry?" Angelique Alea pleaded, even though she knew her words were falling on deaf ears. She knew that Andy wasn't going to speed up, and that bothered her. And what was up with his hygiene? Angelique wrinkled her nose. She wasn't shallow or anything, but Andy looked so awful lately that she was ashamed to be seen with him. He was pallid and his hair was dirty, and that was the same shirt he'd been wearing yesterday.

"Hang on," Andy said, and it seemed to her that he dug through his bag even more slowly, just to annoy her.

Part of her wanted to just leave him standing there, but she waited. They'd been friends for a long time, and they'd been dating for almost a year. But she sure didn't like the way that he was behaving. He didn't care about anything lately, and she was just about sick of it. She'd spoken to him about all of it, and he got a great big attitude, so she'd backed off and given him a little breathing room. Kira dying had been hard on him, and she should remember that. Angelique frowned. But now that she thought about it, all this weirdness had started before Kira died. Ever since he'd met that guy Dan, Andy started acting strange, and she was tired of it. She didn't like that guy, Dan—he just seemed like a big jerk who didn't know what he wanted to do with his life.

Angelique, however, knew perfectly well what she was going to do with hers. And until just recently, Andy had known what he was going to do with his. It didn't matter what she dressed like on the weekends; she did that for fun, and to freak people out. She liked to prove to people that you couldn't tell what someone was like just by looking at them. When you looked at her, in her black, freaky clothing, with her nose ring and her heavy, theatrical makeup, did you think *honor student*? No. But that's what she was. She'd never had a grade lower than an A.

She was going to graduate from FGCU with honors and take her full scholarship right on to medical school. Her Cuban mother told her that she was wasting her time, that she should give up her Goth friends and stop all of her studying. She said that Angelique should just find a good man and marry him, but Angelique didn't listen to her. She loved her mother, but she was from a different generation and she was just too immersed in that submissive Hispanic culture, where the man made all the rules, and the woman took all the orders. That was Old School thinking, that was not today. And Angelique was *definitely* today.

The last thing *she* wanted to do was wind up like her mother, getting married as soon as some man asked her, having a couple of kids and then wondering what happened when her drunken husband took off for who-knows-where and left her with two kids to raise all alone. She wasn't going to scrub toilets for a living, not her. That was not going to happen.

So Angelique did what she wanted to do; partying on the weekends, studying hard every weeknight, making sure that she got the grades that she needed. She was going to have a great life, and nobody was going to give it to her. She would earn it herself.

She stared at Andy now, and wondered why she was bothering with him. She looked at her watch and huffed with displeasure. He was just so *infuriating* lately. Whatever was wrong with him, he'd had long enough and plenty of chances to pull himself out of it. He knew how she felt.

"Maybe you don't care if you're late, but I do," Angelique said. She turned away from him and started down the hall. He shambled after her, catching up just as she opened the door. The teacher shot them a dirty look but didn't say anything, and Angelique considered herself lucky, and made up her mind right then as she headed for a desk. He had been acting this way for weeks. It was time she took her own path. Andy Mossiman could consider himself dumped.

* * *

Dan Jackson stared all around. It was like a different world out here. One hour away from the city, but it was a million miles away from civilization. The humidity seemed ten times worse here than it did in Fort Myers. Marsh grasses grew in profusion, and flamingos and herons stood in the shallow water, their beaks searching the bottom for food. There were more flamingos here in this one spot than he'd seen in his whole life, and Dan had been born in Florida.

Dan cursed as he bogged down momentarily in the silt of the swamp, then pushed off with his oar. He gave a sigh of relief when the boat began to move, propelling himself further into the Everglades. What seemed like millions of mosquitoes buzzed all around him, eating him up despite all the repellant he'd smeared on himself. Hell, he'd even picked up a leech getting into the canoe, and it had left an angry red welt on his leg. Dan shuddered at the thought of the repulsive creature he'd plucked off his leg and tossed overboard. Then he laughed. Here he was, looking down on the leech for being a bloodsucker, but it was just doing the same things he liked to do.

"Isn't that right, Andy?" he called back to the body wrapped in canvas in the back of the canoe, and chuckled at his own wit. "You found that out, didn't you, bud?"

He cackled again and realized he didn't sound quite sane. He'd taken so much of the stuff today; it was hard to know what was real and what wasn't. But hey, sanity was just a word, wasn't it? Dan hadn't really wanted to come out here, but he was Sang's number one man, wasn't he? He had to take care of the problems as they came, and disposing of bodies had come to be a problem. Many more showed up with all the blood gone out of them, and the whole city would be in a panic. It had been his idea to bring them out here to the swamps, and it had been easy enough.

Dan smiled. He'd just bought a canoe *with his money* and put it on top of the car he'd bought with *his* part of the meth money. God, he loved having money. The people who said that money wasn't important had never had to do without it. After all those years of having none, after staying with that miserable, miserly, crazy old woman, it was like being in heaven. And he loved meth. And he loved the ceremonies, and he loved loved *loved* the expression on all of those stupid people's faces when they realized that he'd tricked them. He wanted to laugh when they finally figured out what was coming, and that he'd helped to engineer it all.

After he'd secured the canoe, Dan had stuffed the remains of poor old Andy in the trunk and headed for the Evcrglades. He was really quite clever when he had to be.

Dan heard a low snorting sound and looked around to see a bull alligator slide sinuously down into the water until only his glittering eyes and his nostrils showed. Dan liked alligators; they were as old as the dinosaurs, and they were the kind of cold-blooded killers that he admired. They were killers in the way he imagined the dinosaurs had been before they became extinct; they killed without regret and without feeling. Dan did feel a little regret right now, though; he regretted that Andy Mossiman was already dead. He'd like to cut him a little and toss him in for the gators to feed on. See the frenzy in the water as they fought over him enough to tear him to pieces. Then they'd have dragged him down to drown, screaming, before they shoved him underneath something for a couple of days to ripen and rot. Alligators liked their meat a little *aged.*

Oh, well. Some other time, maybe. Some other victim.

"Here, fella," Dan said softly. "Nice little dinner for you here." And he shoved Andy Mossiman's canvas wrapped body over the side of the canoe, quite sure that no one would ever find it. There would be nothing left to find, anyway. What the gators didn't eat, the other predators would. There might be a piece of bone or two left after they all got done, but who was going to find it out here? The swamp could hide a million bodies if he desired.

* * *

Roland Andrews was pissed. He couldn't believe that he'd been suckered into this. After all that talk last night to his wife about how he was going to be more assertive, how he was going to stop letting people push him around, here he was letting his idiot neighbor talk him into taking him along on one of his trips.

He was a smart man; how did he let these things happen? He'd been one of hundreds of applicants and yet he'd won a grant to further his work, strictly on the strength of his credentials and his proposal. This study he did in the swamps was important, and the data he collected could help them save the wildlife in the Everglades. He couldn't afford to be distracted, and yet he was stuck with this moron for hours now, in a small boat in the middle of nowhere. And it was his own fault.

"Hey, Roland," the idiot called. "Look at all those gators over there. They're sure fightin' over something."

Roland peered through his binoculars at the alligators, and he was sure he saw a flash of something black and red. And it was large. Now what in the hell could that be?

"Hand me that air horn," he said tensely now, pointing to a spot in the boat behind the man. Roland didn't like guns, so he used the air horn to frighten off wildlife when he needed to.

"Just hand it here!" he said impatiently as the man began to ask questions.

He had to blast the horn several times before the alligators began to disperse. They were intent on their prey, and Roland swallowed down bile when he realized what it was that they were fighting over. Usually he loved the fecund smell of the Everglades, but it seemed different now. Fetid; the odor of decay and rot. The smell of death.

Because when they got the boat a little closer, they could tell that the alligators had been fighting over a body. The head and the ragged torso of a young man. Roland's neighbor leaned over the side and vomited when Roland reached out with gloved hands and hauled what was left of the body into the boat.

He was still retching when Roland dialed 911 on the cell phone that he always carried with him when he went into the swamps.

He liked to be prepared, because you never knew when an emergency situation was going to arise.

* * *

Jorge decided to attack the woman that he was following in her own apartment.

He'd been walking down the street, after meeting up with Dan and getting his new supply. He'd already stashed the drugs; but he was too buzzed from checking the batch to stay at home. He just ambled down the street, laughing crazily. He'd go home when he came down a little, when he could stand to be shut behind four walls.

When he saw her come out of the building, he decided right then to do her, just like that. He'd see where she was going, and if he had to, he'd wait. He knew what building she lived in now.

Yeah, he'd do her.

She was tall and blond and plump, just the way he liked them. He started following her right then, followed her right into the grocery store smiling with satisfaction 'cause he knew now that she was going home after she left her. She never even noticed him, 'cause he was way too slick. Jorge was still flying, but he could act straight when he needed to. This was gonna be easy. He didn't see no ring on her finger, so she probably wasn't married. And if she was, or if she had a boyfriend in there shacked up with her, he'd just kill her old man first. Or maybe he'd make the guy watch while he did her.

Jorge waited while she finished up her little grocery shopping, then he followed her home and into the apartment building. It was just as easy as he'd thought it was going to be. And then he showed her his gun and made her take the stairs up to her apartment. He didn't want to get in no elevator, there might be somebody in there and she might scream or something. Not that he was afraid; on the contrary. He wasn't afraid of nobody, but it might get messy, and then he wouldn't get to have his fun.

"Don't make me mad, now," he cautioned her in a slow, creepy voice that made goosebumps pop up on her arms. "You won't like it if you make me mad. But I might." And he giggled in a way that made her shudder.

And she was careful not to make any sudden moves, or try to run away. Maybe it would be okay. He seemed reasonable . . . but she shuddered anyway. He might seem rational, but his eyes gave him away. They were the eyes of a madman, flicking right and left, left and right, and a tic distorted his face every few seconds. And his pupils were so tiny, she could hardly see them. But maybe it would be all right. Maybe it would.

He motioned her into her apartment and stepped in behind her. After they'd both entered, he closed the door and locked it, sliding the deadbolt home. She stood numbly in the tiny foyer, almost paralyzed by panic. Why hadn't she screamed and tried to run? What was she going to do now? What good was a deadbolt if the crazies were already inside the house?

Jorge motioned for her to go into the living room, and a big smile broke over his narrow face when he saw the other girl sitting on the couch. He motioned the girl to sit on the couch with her roommate. He turned on the stereo and a loud beat filled the small room. Jorge smacked his lips as he looked at them, just sitting there and waiting for him, like his two slaves or something.

Mmm-mmm. *Two* blondes with a little wiggle and jiggle to them, he thought. It's my lucky day today. But not theirs.

He was laughing when he walked over to them.

* * *

Jessie was dreaming.

One minute she'd been awake, and the next she was asleep. She hadn't realized that she was so tired, but she must have been. The emotional toll the last week had taken on her had been unbelievable, and it was easy for that to translate to the physical.

Because she was dreaming, and her mother was here. And you had to be asleep to dream. So she must have been tired.

"I've got to tell you a story," her mother said firmly from her cross-legged perch at the end of the bed. ***"And you have to listen, 'kay, baby? It's important."***

"All right," Jessie said. "If it's important. I always liked your stories."

"This one's not mine," Dream-Mom said. ***"It's a story that my Grandmother Belle told me, and she says that she heard it from her Great Grandmother, who told it to her when she was very little."***

"The Grandma Belle that was a full blood Cherokee?" Jessie asked. "She always sounded like so much fun. I always wished I could have met her."

"She says hello," Dream-Mom said. ***"She says that you are brave and beautiful, and that she has met you many times. She says that you see her often in the warmth that shines from a stranger's eyes. And that the blood you share with her knows when she is there, but that she diluted the knowing in all her descendants when she married that no-good stubborn, drunken German. She says that you must trust your heart and not your mind because you put too much faith in what you think is true and do not pay enough attention to what you feel is true."***

Dream-Mom shook her head. ***"No, Grandma, I'm not telling her anything else. I've got to tell her this story, and you keep getting off the subject,"*** she said heatedly to someone that Jessie could not see, even in her dream. And whoever it was must have subsided, because she began her story in a cadence and a manner of speech that was not her own.

> This is the story of a chief who lived long ago. He was wise and brave, this chief, and he was very sad, for his wife had just died and he had no sons or daughters. His wife had often urged him to take a second wife, for it was not right for such a great man to have no sons, but he had resisted. He did not want a second wife, he wanted only her. And so when she died, he was alone.
>
> Now one day, a young woman came riding into camp, her clothes all torn and dirty and her face wild with grief. This young woman was the wife to the chief's brother, and so she was his sister, and the chief honored her as such.
>
> "Help me," she cried. "My husband your brother has been killed by our enemies to the north! They tried, too, to take me prisoner, but I fought them and came here. You must avenge my husband."

When the chief heard this, he took a party of warriors and headed north. The wife of his brother went along, to show them the place where her husband had been killed, and to bring back the body as was proper. But something strange began to happen.

As they rode north, the forest became darker and darker. And though it was summertime, the leaves had already fallen from the trees, and it began to be very cold. And the chief, who was both wise and brave, began to be afraid.

"What witchcraft is this?" he thought, for he had never been afraid before. And all the horses began to shy at the dark shadows in the forest, acting as they do when a great wolf stalks them. And when the chief looked around, he saw that his warriors were afraid, too.

And when he looked at the woman again, he saw that she was not the wife of his brother at all, but a witch in disguise. And the witch called all around her many crows, which cawed horribly. And all of the Cherokee know that the crow is a portent of death.

"What do you want?" the chief asked the witch. "And where is my brother and sister?"

"I have enslaved them," said the witch. "But I will let them go, if you will promise to take their place, for you would make me a much better servant." And she laughed when she said this, for she knew that the chief was proud as well as wise and brave, and that it would be hard for him to act as her servant.

"Very well," said the chief. "But first I must go back to my village and sing my death song with my warriors. For once I come back here, I doubt that I will ever leave."

"Swear to me that you will come back to this very spot one full moon from now," said the witch. "And I will release my prisoners. For I know that your word will not be broken once you give it."

So the chief gave his word, and she released the chief's brother and his wife from her enchantment. The warriors made ready to return to their home and as the chief started to leave, the witch said to him, cackling:

"I have a riddle for you to solve, oh wise one. When you return, answer this question for me, and I will let you go. Otherwise, you will spend the rest of your life in my service. What do women want most in the world and do not know that they already possess?"

The chief and his warriors returned home, and the chief thought to sing his death song right then, but the elders of the tribe convinced him to go and ask everyone of the tribe if they knew the answer to the riddle. And the chief thought that it was a good idea, and he soon found himself with more answers than he wanted.

For every person that he asked gave him a different answer. Some thought the answer was a handsome husband, others a fine teepee with many ponies in the herd, and some told him that the answer to the riddle was numerous fine, brave children. But none of the answers seemed right to the chief and time was growing short, so he asked the elders of the tribe if all the people had given an answer. And it turned out that one woman had not given her answer yet to the chief.

So the day before he was to leave to join the witch as her servant, the wise chief went to seek out this woman, who he found washing clothes on the riverbank. He saw her only from the back first, and he thought that she was a fine figure of a woman, for she was sleek and muscled and strong as she did her work. Then she turned around and the chief saw that she was the ugliest woman that he had ever seen.

Her hair was the texture of a horse's tail, and it surrounded a face that was the color of rancid fat. Her eyes were too close together and very small, and her nose was flattened on her face. Her teeth were huge as a horse's teeth, and they stuck out between her lips even when she closed her mouth, and she seemed to have no chin.

"I know the answer to the riddle," she told him. "But I have a request of you. You must take me as your wife, for my entire family was killed and I have no kin. I have to rely on others to provide for me, and I want a home of my own."

And the chief agreed, without hesitating.

The next morning the chief rode north to meet the witch, and he found her there in the very spot that he had left her.

"Well," she cackled. "Tell me the answer to the riddle, or humble yourself as my servant."

And the chief told her what the ugly woman had said.

"The answer to your riddle is this: Women want the power to rule over men, but they already have it."

And the witch screamed horribly, loud and long, and stamped her feet. Crows came cawing around her, lifting her by her garments and carrying her away, for she knew that she had lost and would have no servant here. For this was the true answer to the riddle. Women often rule over men without even knowing that it is so.

The chief went home to prepare for a wedding, for he had given his word to the ugly woman. The elders of his tribe tried to talk the chief into marrying another, for they said that the woman was unsuitable. But the chief was adamant. It would be so.

At their wedding feast, all were uneasy at the bad match that they thought their chief had made. The bride sat proudly beside her new husband, her sallow cheeks flushed red with embarrassment, for she could hear the comments that the other women made loudly about her.

“She is ugly and old,” said one. “She can never give him children.”

“It’s a wonder she doesn’t whinny instead of speaking,” said another. “With those teeth, I would expect it.”

“She is not worthy of him,” said yet another. “She should be ashamed for forcing this marriage upon him.”

And the chief kept his silence and ignored the chattering of the women until he saw that his bride’s tiny eyes were shining dark with tears.

“Silence!” he thundered to them all. “You say that she is old, but does not wisdom and dignity come with age? Are these not good qualities for a wife to possess? Do you think that honor is found in the teeth, or is it found in the heart? Is the character of a woman to be found in her face, or in her actions? Honor my choice, my people, for this is she, and I will not deny my wife because you think that I must.”

And the people felt ashamed because they knew that everything that he said was good and true and that they had behaved badly toward his new bride.

"You are right in everything that you say," they told the chief. "And we welcome your bride."

"Thank you," cried his bride, and while they looked upon her, her face began to change. She became beautiful; her hair grew long and silky, and her skin clear and dewy. She had straight, white teeth between lips as red as strawberries, and her eyes were as brown and large as a doe's. She had a pointed little chin and a fine straight nose, and all stared in astonishment.

"I, too, was under an enchantment from the witch," she explained. "And only if I could find a man who could see past the ugliness of my features to the beauty of my heart would I ever be freed."

And the chief and his tribe rejoiced in the good marriage that he had made, and he and his new bride lived a long and happy life, and had many brave sons and beautiful daughters.

But there was something that the wise chief never told his wife or his tribe. After the witch had tricked him by disguising herself as his brother's wife, he had gone to the medicine man, who taught him to see beneath the outer self of a person to the soul beneath. So he had known all along that his bride-to-be was beautiful.

"There is something that you need to know about this story," Dream-Mom said. ***"The chief in the story was your ancestor, and he has given every one of his lineage the ability to see through those who masquerade as something else."***

Dream-Mom grasped Jessie's hand hard.

"You can see through any disguise, so remember that. Grandma Belle says to look with the eyes underneath your eyes, and to be careful. He is even more dangerous than the witch was, because he will not keep any promises that he makes. He has no honor and no fear because he has no soul."

Jessie yawned and went downstairs for a glass of iced tea. She needed the caffeine jolt to help her wake up after that strange dream.

CHAPTER FOUR

Lightning flashed jaggedly, bisecting the purple-black clouds in the hazy twilight sky. Gusting winds tugged at the palm fronds and sent leaves whipping through the air. Jessie stared moodily out the window with her chin in her hands. Rain beat down hard on the roof, hitting so hard that it sounded like hail. It suited Jessie's mood.

It was Mrs. Davis' bridge night, and she wouldn't be home until at least ten. Jessie didn't know if that was a relief or a sorrow. She didn't want to be alone; but she didn't want to be with anyone, either. Shannon was driving her crazy, because every time she tried to talk to her about Kira's death, she brushed her off. She kept saying that it was over and done with, and that it was time to move on with life. And she'd never look Jessie in the eyes while she was saying it.

Jessie sighed. Maybe she'd soak in a nice hot bath, with some bath salts. She was halfway down the hall when the phone rang, and she tensed. Maybe it was the psycho calling back again.

There was no answer at the other end of the phone when she picked it up. She hung up with a slam, and stood there frowning. How had this clown got her number, anyway? She hadn't thought of it before, but it had to be somebody who knew her, because how else would they know that she lived with Mrs. Davis? It wasn't like she listed it in the school paper or something, or went around telling everybody.

And at that moment, all the lights in the house blinked out.

Jessie stood in the hall, feeling the wave of darkness washing over her. She could feel her heart begin to beat faster and fear flooded her body. Then she told herself not to be silly. There was a storm outside, wasn't there? And the electricity always went out during a storm. She'd just go downstairs and find the candles that Mrs. Davis kept for emergencies. She groped her way toward the staircase, and carefully holding on to the railing, began to descend into the blackness. Then she saw a thin beam of light bobbing around downstairs.

"Mrs. Davis?" she called out waveringly. "Is that you?" Her voice echoed in the big house, and the thin beam of light turned toward her.

And nobody answered her.

Mrs. Davis would have answered. So who was it? Jessie's heart pounded hard and her legs felt weak. She turned and went back up the stairs as quickly as she could, and hurried to her room. She locked herself in. What was she going to do? Jessie backed away from the door. Her phone was cordless and the electricity was out, so that wouldn't work. Where had she left her cell phone?

It was in her purse. She rummaged desperately around on the floor, her eyes adjusting to the dim light. Where was it? She finally found the purse shoved underneath the edge of the bed, and her fingers had just closed on the cell phone when she saw the doorknob begin to move.

Jessie froze. The door shook as somebody on the other side rattled it, and she heard a low laugh.

"I told you to stay out of it," said a voice. "I told you, didn't I?"

"I'm calling the cops!" Jessie screamed. "I'm calling them right now!"

There was another laugh outside her door. "I'm leaving now," the voice said. "Call them if you want. And just think, Jessie, this door is locked, but it's flimsy. I could have gotten in here if I wanted to. So do as you're told and stop asking questions."

Jessie stayed tensely crouched on the floor, watching the doorknob, but it never turned again and she didn't hear anything else. And a few minutes later, the power came back on. She turned on all the lights, and Mrs. Davis exclaimed at the brightness when she got home. The little old lady went around turning them all off, but Jessie slept with a nightlight that night.

She didn't tell Mrs. Davis about the intruder, either.

* * *

"Jessie!" Mrs. Davis called, and the hoarse sound of her voice sent Jessie flying down the stairs.

"What is it?" she called, frightened. "Mrs. Davis, what is it?"

Sergeant Bennett stood in the open doorway, and Jessie raced up to put her arm around Mrs. Davis, supporting her. She glared indignantly at the police officer.

"What are you doing here?" she asked coldly.

"I have all the necessary papers to search your house," he said. "I am not here alone, there are six patrolmen with me. Let me in, please. I have the law on my side." Mrs. Davis made a little snorting noise. He flushed a little as he met the scornful gaze of the older woman.

"Look," he said more softly. "We're not going to tear up your stuff, regardless of what you see on TV. We're just going to look around. At most you'll have things to put away when we're done."

"You're fooling yourself, and you're wasting time," Jessie said furiously as he handed her the warrant. "I don't take drugs and I don't know anything about any meth. Why don't you go find the real killer instead of bothering me?"

They moved reluctantly out of his way. His sharp eyes noted as she helped Mrs. Davis to a chair and fussed over her a little, bringing her a pillow to lean on and a hassock to prop her feet up on.

"I didn't have anything to do with this. Kira was hanging out with a bunch of Goth kids. They might know something about all of this stuff, because she was going to some kind of Goth party that Friday."

"Why didn't you tell me this before?" he asked sharply. "It's against the law to withhold information. You could have ... "

"Because you made her angry," Mrs. Davis said crisply. "And she forgot. Just as you're making us both angry now, treating her as a suspect. *She forgot.* It's not a hanging offense, and she'd just found out that her best friend was dead. Look, sergeant, can't you see that this is ridiculous? This is a child who's had a stunning loss in the last few months. Not just her mother, but her best friend was killed. There is some kind of monster going around killing at random, and you are bothering the one person who has been the victim in this crime as surely as the two who were murdered."

Sergeant Bennett looked at the floor momentarily.

"There's been another murder," he said, bringing his head up to meet Jessie's eyes. "It's someone else you know. It's Andy Mossiman."

And Jessie fainted.

"There's something evil happening, baby."

She was dreaming that Mom was sitting on the couch again, only this time her arms were wrapped warmly around Jessie, who reveled in the touch. She could remember sitting like this so many nights with Mom. They'd be watching TV, or just talking, but Mom always had to be touching. She used to say that she was some kind of changeling, along with her sister Lucy, because nobody else in her family touched each other unless they had to. But her and Lucy, she always said, they just had to be snuggled up like little kittens all the time, and Jessie was the same way. She didn't feel right unless she got her ten hugs every day. Mom was talking again, so Jessie tried to pay attention, but it was hard. She just felt so warm and kind of . . . float-y, if that was a word.

"It's gonna get worse, honey," Mom said gravely. ***"And you might find out that people you trust can betray you. But I'm here, and I can help. You just have to call."***

"How can you help?" Jessie asked. "You're just a dream. It's nice that you're here, but I'm only dreaming."

"Remember what I said," Dream-Mom said. ***"Wake up now, and talk to this man. He's not as bad as he seems. He can help."***

And her caressing hand left Jessie's hair and Jessie could have cried with the loss of the warmth.

"Mom?" she said, and opened her eyes to stare into Sergeant Bennett's grave gaze as he leaned over her. Jessie sat up on the couch where she was lying and looked around groggily.

"I'm okay now, Mrs. Davis," she said quickly, and wiped away the tears that just didn't seem to want to stop flowing. Silently, Sergeant Bennett handed her the tissues from the end table, and she rubbed her eyes. "Don't get upset. It just ... it just ... "

"Oh, Jessie," the little woman said sadly, plumping herself down beside the girl and hugging her close. Mrs. Davis needed a lot of hugs and touching, too. "I think that we need to talk to this policeman. Maybe we do know something that will help."

But it turned out that they had nothing much to add to the investigation, after all, besides the things that Jessie had already told him. Jessie knew Andy Mossiman, and had even dated him for a little while in high school, but she hadn't been deeply involved with his life. He was a sweet, smart boy, who liked to restore old cars, watch Star Trek, and play games on his computer. Other than that, she didn't really know anything about him. He hung out mostly with his girlfriend Angelique and her friends. Sergeant Bennett scribbled a little in his little notebook, but Jessie figured he was faking it. Mostly, he nibbled at the cookie he'd been given, as Mrs. Davis was never happier than when feeding someone.

Evidently, he'd displayed enough regret when Jessie had fainted from the shock of his announcement to placate Mrs. Davis. He was definitely in her good graces, to judge from the admiring little glances she kept throwing him. And another good indication that Mrs. Davis had changed her mind about the policeman was the 'good cookie' he was eating, because she refused to get out her 'good cookies' for people she didn't care for. Jessie always knew immediately which of her friends Mrs. Davis liked and which she didn't, just from the cookies they were offered.

The patrolmen had all gone home except one, who had been left behind to put away the things they had taken out. They'd found nothing, of course. Jessie wasn't sure if it was standard procedure to clean things up after a search, but she kind of doubted it. The young patrolman sure hadn't seemed happy about having to do it.

"Andy's body was found way back in the Everglades by a biologist doing research. Whoever dumped it there just got unlucky," the cop said now around his cookie. "It appears that it had been dumped just that day, otherwise it would have been eaten already by some of the wildlife. As it was, there's not a whole lot left. The biologist found it because he saw two alligators fighting over it, and he called the police on his cell phone. We're waiting on an autopsy now, but I expect to find that he's full of methamphetamines, too."

Jessie winced. Maybe Sergeant Bennett was trying to be nicer, but he sure wasn't any good at it. She could have done without the visual.

“Are you sure that you don’t know anything about the methamphetamines?” he asked her urgently. “Maybe some of your friends told you about it, or tried to sell you some? Think hard, now. This is important.”

He held up a hand when Mrs. Davis began to bristle. “I’m not accusing her,” he said quickly. “But there’s been a rash of people admitted into emergency rooms lately with overdoses. It’s mostly young people, and the overdoses are all methamphetamines. We think there’s a new lab here somewhere close. I’m just trying to do my job.”

When the young cop stuck his head into the kitchen and told the Sergeant that he was done, Bennett looked happy to leave. Mrs. Davis had become decidedly more cool towards him. Jessie went to let them out, then lingered by the front door after she’d shut it when she heard the conversation begin on the porch steps.

“You think they’re ever gonna solve these?” she heard the young cop ask. “Because it sure don’t seem to me that you got much to go on.”

Sergeant Bennett sighed heavily.

“You’re right about that, Corey,” he said, and Jessie strained to hear as their voices got further away. “We don’t have much to go on. And I won’t be looking too hard for more evidence. I think that these people got in the way of some crazy meth-head and he made an example of them. Maybe they thought that they could sell in some guy’s territory, I don’t know. They were all using, that’s for sure.” Jessie trembled and burned with the force of her anger as his last comment floated back to her. “Nobody cares much about drug addicts, including me.”

* * *

Jessie hadn’t been sleeping well, and it started to catch up with her. She found herself daydreaming in class, her thoughts just wandering away, and once she'd nodded off during Biology 1, which was usually her favorite subject. So when her eyes began to drift closed during some boring sitcom she'd agreed to watch with Mrs. Davis, Jessie decided to give it up and go to bed. Who cared if it was only eight o'clock? If she was tired, she was tired. She barely got her clothes off and tumbled onto the bed before she was asleep. She never even turned her light off, and she didn't stir when Mrs. Davis came in and turned it off for her, covering her up with the sheet that lay tangled at the bottom of the bed.

The doorbell woke her. Jessie stumbled up and looked at the clock. 12:30. She wrapped a robe around herself and went down the stairs, still groggy, holding onto the rail. Who was coming over at this time of the night? If it was one of her friends, they were really going to hear about it, because they sure didn't need to wake Mrs. Davis up. She needed her rest.

Jessie wrenched the door open without even looking through the peephole to see who it was. If Mrs. Davis had been awake, she would have scolded her for sure. A man was standing in the entrance, and she stared at him, speechless.

He was beautiful.

He had hair that was the same silvery-blond that women often try to get out of a bottle and rarely succeed, winding up with a pale imitation. Eyes a startling pale blue, the color of the sky on a cloudless day. He had a patrician nose, and a high forehead, and his mouth was a lush, startling red against the pearl of his skin. His suit was impeccably tailored and fit his perfect form impeccably. Jessie could smell the cologne that he had put on his skin, and it smelled divine. Then as she took a deep breath, trying to draw in that gorgeous scent, she frowned. There seemed a nasty undertone to this cologne, as if it covered something vile ... something rotten. He extended a hand toward Jessie, who took it automatically. His hand was cool, almost cold, and she dropped it with a shudder that she couldn't disguise.

"Hi," he said winsomely, smiling brightly. "I'm doing a follow-up on the investigation into your mother's death. I'd like to come in and ask you a few questions, if I may."

Jessie clutched her robe around herself. Her hand burned where she had touched his, and she rubbed it against her thigh. His eyes followed the movement, and she felt strangely uneasy.

"It's too late," she said firmly. "Mrs. Davis is asleep, and so was I until you rang the doorbell. You need to come back in the daytime."

She saw a flash of something, only a flash, on his face. He dropped that sincere, pleasant smile and betrayed his fury, a ghastly expression of anger so deep that Jessie fell back a step. The shocking expression was gone so quickly that Jessie thought she might have imagined it. Because he was smiling again, so pleasantly, so hypnotically. He glanced at the gold watch on his arm, and Jessie wondered, was that a Rolex? What was a government employee doing with a Rolex?

"I am sorry, it is late. I hadn't realized how late until just now. You can't imagine how many hours a week I put in, and the time just got away from. I have so much to do. Perhaps if you invited me in, I could just take a peek around and see what your home looks like. I'm well aware of the facts of the case, Jessie, and this won't take me long at all. I could take this off my list of things to do, if you just invited me in now."

Jessie was strangely tempted to let him in. His smile was so sincere, and she knew he did have a lot to do. They were all overworked, police officers were, she'd found that out when her mother died. She didn't know how they got all of their work done. And at least this guy was polite, unlike some of the other cops she'd met lately.

He leaned forward. "Please, Jessie," he said in a soft, intimate voice. "I'm a very busy person and I have so much to do. This would help me out so much."

She opened her mouth to tell him, yes, it would be okay, and a familiar voice screamed suddenly in her head.

"Don't do it, baby! No, he ain't what he seems, you got to tell him no, no matter what. Say no, right now. Say no!"

"No," she said abruptly. "No, you can't come in, it's too late. Come back during the day." She started to swing the door shut. He put a hand on the door, holding it open, and Jessie felt a cold fear touch her as she met his glittering eyes. The rage on his face was undisguised now, and she choked at the force of it battering against her.

"I'll be back then," he said softly. "I'll be back."

He took his hand off the door, and Jessie slammed it shut, then stood scant seconds with her back against it, trembling. Then she turned and locked it quickly and fell against it again, her heart pounding, and she could have sworn that she heard a low chuckle right outside. But she was too afraid to put her eye to the peephole to see if he was still there.

Only after her pulse returned to normal did she realize that the man who claimed to be a policeman hadn't told her his name. And she hadn't seen an unfamiliar car on the street. How had he arrived at the house? Buses quit running at nine o'clock, and it was well after midnight. Did he walk from his downtown office? That was miles away.

Jessie went to bed, but it took her hours to go to sleep, and her dreams were peopled with beautiful men who turned into monsters with glowing red eyes when you didn't give them what they wanted.

* * *

He was wearied and enraged as he walked down the sidewalk. It should have been a rapid and certain revenge but it hadn't been, and the girl had escaped. She should not have been able to resist him, he had turned the full force of his powers on her, and she had been giving in, when that ... presence had come between them. It was very vexing, that presence. It had formed a psychic wall between him and his prey, and he had been forced to leave.

He would have his reprisal. He would take it slowly, and it would be delicious. He had to remember that when dealing with an unknown power, one must pull back and take stock, perhaps come back with reinforcements, even though all his instincts had said to attack her now, take her now, kill the threat *now.*

He hadn't expected to come across such a danger, but he was prepared now. He would find out about this presence, and he would obliterate it, and that girl would be made to suffer the terrors of the damned because he had to wait. He did not like to wait ...

He walked through the streets, anger whipping, his belly filling with a crude appetite. Desperate hunger. His senses were heightened to their peak, and he could smell the blood of the creatures in their houses and their cars. His nostrils flared and it was all he could do not to rip open the metal monstrosities and pull out its passengers, screaming, and devour them whole. Only the thought that there were safer ways of sating himself kept him from doing so. Safer prey, and it was close.

He found the prey he had sensed, and he was lying, asleep, behind a garbage can in an alley. Paper bag with a liquor bottle clutched tightly by his side, even in his sleep. The man who now called himself Sang Adorer smiled as he looked down on the filthy man. He would be doing the world a favor by ridding it of such trash. This man was obviously not an important member of society. He wouldn't be missed, and that was just what Sang needed right now. Someone who wouldn't be missed.

"Hello," he said quietly, nudging the drunk awake with one immaculate shoe, being careful of course not to dirty it in the garbage that lay all around him. He smiled when the bum half opened his eyes.

"Wha' you want, man?" the bum asked sleepily. "I'm just tryin' to get some rest here."

"I'm not a man," Sang Adorer said gently, and he was on him before the man could make another sound, severing his windpipe with his sharp fangs. Rich, warm blood flooded into his mouth, and the bum quivered and gurgled in his grasp. Sang grasped him securely until he stopped wriggling and sucked at every drop of the rich blood. Lapped up every bit of the wine-tainted ambrosia. Sometimes when you had glutted many times on the finest of vintages, you hungered for a lesser wine. Something a little more common, as an appetizer. He threw the remains to one side when he was done, behind the garbage cans, after ripping the throat open just a little more with his fangs, and biting the body in a couple more places. There, now perhaps this would fool his friends the police. It looked as if a dog had been at the corpse.

And in seconds, Sang Adorer was out on the sidewalk and on his way, searching for his next victim.

"Hey, there," a shadow said, coming away from the wall and turning into the figure of a young girl as the shadow came closer. "Care for a little company?"

"Perhaps," Sang said smoothly, his eyes coming up to meet hers, ignoring her slight gasp.

She was hardly his type, this lady of the night, but what the hell, he was slumming tonight. She was wearing a short skirt, and her blouse was so low cut that her breasts were spilling from it. It made for easy access for her customers, which was important since she often did it in cars or even in the alley when her johns didn't want to pay for a place. She was barely out of her teens, and she was a bit heavy of hip and breast, but her features weren't too bad. And she was clean, which was more than could be said for the one he had just left.

"Hey, maybe I changed my mind," the girl said nervously and cried out as Sang reached out a long finger and ran the nail slowly, slowly down the bare skin of her arm, drawing blood. "Why don't you go on down the street and find somebody else, mister?"

"So warm," he murmured as he licked her essence off of his fingernail. "I think that you will do, my dear. You will do for me just fine."

And as he drug her into the shadows of the alley, laughing, never releasing her eyes from his gaze, the fleshy young prostitute never made a sound louder than a whimper.

Even when, on impulse, he reached out and tore her wisp of a blouse open with both hands to free her breasts to his eyes. Sang gave a soft laugh as she struggled with him, her naked breasts bouncing and her nipples rising as he gazed upon them.

He touched her with his mind and forced her to his will, and it was easy to do. She struggled briefly in the bonds of his intellect, but he quickly overpowered her. He felt a moment's regret at the ease of it; it was so much more fun if it was difficult, if they had an intricate, perplexing structure to their mind. She slowly took a step toward him, and even more slowly reached out to touch him. Her hand slid over his face and inside his shirt to caress his chest. He held very still, only turning his head to nip at her palm, sucking briefly on the blood, throwing back his head at the ecstasy of it. Her hand slid lower and undid the button of his pants and slid inside to cup him in her hands. She fondled him expertly, and he groaned softly. It had been a long time since he mixed sex with blood, and he had forgotten the thrill of it.

She edged closer to him, then found herself pulled into an embrace, found herself kissed in a way that sent blood rushing hot to every extremity. Somewhere inside herself she knew and was horrified at what was happening, but she had no control over herself. The hunger shuddered inside her with every throbbing beat of her heart. She kissed him back with desperation, feeling his fangs nick her but not caring, and her mouth filled with blood. He sucked it from her warmth frantically, sensuously. His hands kneaded roughly at her naked flesh, squeezed her breasts roughly while she squirmed against him. He tore her skirt and panties from her, and she rejoiced, making little desperate sounds when his hands molded her to him, when his fingers brutally entered her every orifice, when he slammed her against the brick wall and ground harshly against her.

She threw her head back and screamed silently when he cupped her ample buttocks in his hands, lifted her up, and impaled her on his hardness. It hurt, oh, it hurt, and yet it was also an exquisite pleasure that she would not have given up for all the gold in the city. He was cold and thick inside her as he held her hips and thrust cruelly, and the rest of the world seemed to be just shadows and mist around her. She existed only for this, only to please her master, and she wrapped her legs around him and rose and fell desperately on him, rode him hard despite the pain as he sucked at her neck, sucked her life from her body.

He was everything she had ever wanted, sleek and agile, his flesh searing her with its cold burn, her body sensitized beyond belief by the plunging flesh inside her. She had been destined for this moment, it was the only reason she had even been born. Merely to serve his body. She drifted on a wave of sensation so intense that she felt she couldn't bear it, and she lost all thought except that of fucking him. And yet, in a brief moment of sanity, she realized that she was deep in carnal pleasure with something that was not quite human and she was moving desperately toward a fulfillment that was sure to mean her death.

Then all thought was gone, and he swelled inside her, becoming so big that she felt as if he would tear her apart. She felt a fluid heat coming from him into her, and she burned and yet felt cold from the center of her being to the ends of her fingertips. She felt that she was ablaze with cold fire from the inside out, and that she would go up in flames at any second. He filled her, hard and strong, exploding inside her, lapping and suckling ferociously at her smooth neck as he jerked her frantically up and down. And then she exploded too, her body pulsing around his, gripping him with the strong young muscles of her vagina, and she thought hazily, weakly, that she had never come like that before, not realizing that she never would again because she was nearly dead.

Sang Adorer held her dying body still on his throbbing shaft, licking the last few drops of blood from his lips, and he giggled as her head flopped grotesquely to one side. When he was sure that she was completely gone, he carefully removed her from his still throbbing flesh and put her tenderly down onto the ground. Who knew that the grubby little whore would be so hot? If he had but known, he would have kept her to play with for a while. Of course, it was too late now. At least she had died giving him ecstasy.

Sated, he laughed, feeling powerful and euphoric. He was glutted and glowing with the blood of the two victims he had just claimed, and he knelt to stroke the girl's blond hair tenderly as she stared vacantly up at the sky.

"Goodbye, child," he said. "I wonder what your name was?"

He laughed again as he left her lying there in the alley. They all had names, he was sure, but who could keep track of them? He headed briskly for home, aware that it would soon be dawn. He needed sleep. He thought idly that he would tell Dan to bring him only women from now on. He really did deserve the pleasure, and they all died so happy. But perhaps the next time he would forgo the control of her mind and let her struggle and squeal beneath him while he conquered her physically. Sometimes he liked it that way; their ineffectual struggles increased his pleasure. He liked it that way, too, oh yes he did.

CHAPTER FIVE

In the morning, it all felt different to Jessie. Her fears from the night before seemed silly, he was just an overworked civil servant, not a monster. He'd probably parked his car a block away or something, and then walked up. And that flash of ... rage ... she'd seen on his face, well, that was probably just her imagination. She did have a big imagination, after all.

Still, Jessie felt threatened enough that she needed to talk to somebody about it, so she cornered Shannon after her first class and told her what had happened. She was stunned by her friend's reaction. Shannon paled and swayed, and then she leaned her head into Jessie, first looking around to see if anyone watched.

"I've got to tell you something," she whispered. "Let's ditch class and go to the library where we can talk."

When they huddled at a table in the far corner of the library and Jessie heard what her friend had to say, she felt as if she were still in one of her dreams from the night before.

"Listen," Shannon said intensely, "no matter what time this man comes, don't let him in, Jessie. He's not a policeman; he's something else. He's not who he claims to be. His name is Sang Adorer."

"How do you know?" Jessie asked in surprise.

"I ... I just do," Shannon said. "I found some stuff out. Jessie, I know you're not going to believe me and I swore I wouldn't tell you this, but I want you think about this all for a minute."

"Your Mom and Andy and Kira, when they were killed, they all had something in common, right?"

"They were all mutilated, and they all tested positive for methamphetamines, yes," Jessie said. "You think this guy who came to the house last night had something to do with it?" She leaned forward, suddenly excited. "What did you find out, Shannon? I know that you were going to talk to some of your Goth friends, what'd they say?"

"*No*," Shannon hissed. "Not the drugs. And they weren't mutilated. They were missing a lot of blood. *They were slashed to increase the flow of blood from their body.*"

"What are you talking about?" Jessie said in horror. "You mean they're using people in some sort of blood rites, or something, and that's why all these people have died? Because these crazy people want to pretend that they're vampires or something, so they kill people and drink their blood?"

"Ssshh," Shannon said. "Keep your voice down. Some of them aren't pretending, Jessie. Some of them are for real."

Not wanting to hurt her friend and wishing she could avoid this ridiculous topic, Jessie stared at her for a long moment without saying a word. Shannon was nearly the color of milk, she was so white, and her hands were shaking badly. Obviously she believed this, and Jessie just couldn't think of anything to say. She cleared her throat and opted for the bald truth.

"You've got to be kidding me. Are you saying that this guy, this Sang Adorer is a real vampire? That's the most ridiculous thing I've ever heard. I'm not saying that I couldn't be persuaded that some of the supernatural is real, but I'm certainly not going to believe there are undead people who drink blood. All the stress is getting to you, and they've got you buying into their sick fantasy. Come on, the man's not even wearing a cape."

"Don't be facetious," Shannon said intently. "I'm not kidding, and it's not funny. I did some research on this guy, and guess what? He's not from France. He's not from anywhere. And the name Sang Adorer is French for Blood Worship."

"So he's some wacko." Jessie was uncomfortable with the light in Shannon's eyes. "He's just some weird little man with a blood fetish. He made up a name and he got some other wackos to join him, and they all take drugs and kill people. He's not a vampire, Shannon. You're flipping out."

"NO!" Shannon grabbed Jessie's arm with surprising strength and her eyes flashed with a temper that frightened her, that made Jessie feel cold right down to the bone.

Jessie was dizzy all of a sudden, and the room began to spin. Horrified, she realized that she was hallucinating; she began to be able to see beneath Shannon's skin. She could see the veins and the arteries that snaked through the arm that touched her, and Jessie looked up slowly, until her eyes were focused on Shannon's chest. She could see the heart beating there: thump-thump, thump-thump, and she could see all the way inside to the chambers of the heart. Jessie recoiled in horror when she saw what was lying there, and Shannon shook her furiously. Jessie closed her eyes and when she opened them, she was relieved to find out that she could no longer see through Shannon's skin.

"What's wrong with you? You're not taking this seriously, and you should. You're in mortal danger. He's not a joke, and he's not a crazy. He's a vampire, a horrible monster. He's a murderer who preys on his own kind, and he must be stopped. And there is someone else you should know about. His name is Dan Jackson, and he works at a hotel down on the beach. It's called The Beach Bum. He's the one that invited Kira to the party, and Andy Mossiman was real friendly with him right before he died."

Shannon leaned forward suddenly and hugged Jessie fiercely, not seeming to notice that Jessie was stiff in her arms and did her best to hold herself away from Shannon's body.

"I've got to go now. Be careful, Jessie."

And Jessie stared, bemused, as Shannon walked away with her dark hair bouncing and her lush hips swaying. Everything seemed so normal, but Jessie felt like she was caught in a nightmare and couldn't wake up. Shannon had never acted like this before.

She'd always been one of the most even-tempered people Jessie had ever known. She was always slow to anger, had been ever since Jessie had known her, but when she had argued with her, she'd actually thought for a moment that Shannon was going to attack her. And Jessie refused to believe that the hallucination she'd had about the thing she had seen inside Shannon's heart had anything to do with the change in her temperament.

It had been a delusion, caused by stress and lack of sleep. It hadn't been real.

Because she couldn't see through people's skins and there couldn't really be a worm living in Shannon's heart.

A worm as coal black as midnight.

Deaths and mutilation and vampires and blood rites. What the hell was happening around here? Just a few months ago, the only thing on all their minds was how to get to a beach party on Friday night. Now look at them.

Jessie decided that while she was here she would check the various volumes having to do with witchcraft and vampires and other aspects of the black arts. There were plenty of them, because people have always been attracted to the occult, and she sat poring over the titles, her fascination with them absorbing all her attention.

One reference in particular written by a leading master of the subject was about vampirism and a form of Black Mass.

> The Black Mass is still with us, and I have come across a form that promotes evil and evil behavior. I am not speaking of Wicca, for their beliefs are very different from this sect. Even in this age, there are active groups of this type of Satanists in every country. I have heard of them in London, and Paris, and New York, and in more out-of-the-way places in many other countries. They have secret signs and meeting places, and they practice strict secrecy of the identity of their members. It is not the drugs, the black clothing, the black candles, or the black wine that disturbs me about these gatherings ... it is the drinking of what I am told is human blood ... and the blood is always better, one member told me, when it is drawn from an unwilling subject. There was a hint from my source that the subjects were killed in order to draw their blood ...

Jessie felt cold wave down her spine, and the hair on the back of her neck stood up. She slammed the book shut with a bang that echoed through the quiet of the library, earning a glare from the librarian who sat at the desk reading. Jessie ignored her and rose to her feet to return the book to its place on the shelf.

She was going to make Shannon go with her to the Beach Bum after her classes were over, if she thought this guy Dan Jackson was so important. Whatever was happening here was just too scary to go through alone.

Shannon finally agreed to go, but she acted weird the whole time. She fidgeted in the car, seeming unable to sit still, and she kept glancing behind them. Jessie finally yelled at her because she was making her nervous, and Shannon had another of those flashes of temper that had so frightened Jessie before. Shannon's lips drew away from her teeth as she glared at Jessie, looking so predatory and out of control that Jessie felt a moment of pure fright. Then in a flash Shannon's expression changed, and she apologized, telling Jessie that she was just exhausted and scared by all of this. Since Jessie knew exactly how she felt, she forgave her. Hey, who could help acting a little strange with all this stuff going on?

They told the manager of the hotel, a greasy little man who reminded Jessie of a weasel, that they were looking for Dan to tell him that a friend of his had been killed. They didn't know him personally, but their friend had spoken of Dan a lot, and they felt that he should know. He told them that Dan had quit two weeks ago. He did, however, have Dan's address if they were interested. That is, if they would tell the little bastard that there was no way he was getting his last check. Not after he'd left him so short handed that he, personally, had to cover two of his shifts. He pointed to a picture hanging on the wall, with a plaque underneath it that said employee of the month. The face in it was innocent and ingenuous, with freckles smeared all over his features and an endearing little grin that made you just want to squeeze him. He looked like somebody that Jessie knew, but she couldn't place who it was, and she said as much.

"Yeah, that's what made him so good around here," the manager said. "He looks like somebody *everybody* knows. He was great at first. I thought I'd hit the jackpot. He showed up on time, all the customers liked him, he did his job well. I always expected to lose him eventually, but I thought it would be to some bigger place who could pay him more money, and that he'd do the right thing and give notice at least. Not leave me in the lurch."

And he swatted the paper he held in his hands at the desk, irritably. "Turns out he was just like all the rest of the jerks around here."

Shannon refused to have anything else to do with any more investigating. She told Jessie that whatever else she wanted to do, she could do it on her own. Jessie decided she'd wait until tomorrow to go by Dan Jackson's home, because Mrs. Davis would worry if she were too late coming home. She'd talk to Shannon about it later and try to browbeat her into helping. It had always worked with Shannon before, so why change up now?

Jessie had already dropped Shannon off at her house when she realized who Dan Jackson reminded her of. He looked like the kid who played on that show she'd seen in reruns, the one from the 80's, the guy that went on to direct all kinds of movies. Happy Days, that was it. That was who Dan Jackson reminded her of. He looked like Ron Howard did when he played on Happy Days.

* * *

Heather Baker liked to sit in her backyard after dark; it was so peaceful then. She liked the patterns that the moonlight made on her lawn furniture; she liked the quiet of the night.

"I hate the city during the day," she'd often told her husband. "If I couldn't sit outside at night and listen to the silence I'd have moved to the country long ago. It's the time when magic is possible."

Her husband Stan was used to her eccentricities and only nodded. Sometimes he stayed awake with her, but not tonight. He'd fallen asleep on the couch watching TV and she'd woken him with a nudge. Then he'd stumbled off to bed and she'd come outside to watch the night once more.

The moonlight was suddenly dimmed by a black wisp of cloud that floated across it. Heather looked up frowning, and realized that someone else was in the yard with her. She could dimly see his outline against the orange tree. Her heart jumped in her chest. Then for some unknown reason, she felt peace wash through her, and she was suddenly not afraid.

She stood up and drifted over to the dim figure, and she smiled when she got closer. It was a man, and he was the most gorgeous person she had ever seen. She put out a hand to touch the smooth, cool silk of his shirt, rubbing her palm against the firm muscle of his chest. Heather didn't wonder why he was here, suddenly in her back yard, because she knew. He was magic; the magic in the night that she had always waited for.

"Hello," she said softly. "And who are you?"

Suddenly, unexpectedly, without a word spoken between them, he began to kiss her—fiercely, violently, bending her body back while he held her wrists pinioned behind her so that she was helpless to resist him. He ripped at her clothing until she stood naked before him. His lips and fingers searched her, explored her everywhere. But Heather had no thought of resisting. She was caught in the web of his dark sorcery, and she liked the things that he was doing to her. He forced her down onto the ground on her back.

Like a sleepwalker she lay there, feeling the roughness of his clothing against her skin, exciting her. She felt drugged, somehow, the moonlight shining into her eyes until she was forced to close them. The heavy scent of the orange blossoms cascaded over her, making her head swim. He slid down over her naked body, his tongue licking and biting at her breasts, at her navel, until at last he stopped between her thighs, driving her so crazy that she jerked around, whimpering, and arched her back in uncontrollable passion. When Stan did this, she liked it, but this was different somehow. It was a *violation*, but it was a violation that she longed for desperately. Even when he nicked her with his teeth and she felt him sucking at the blood there, she was excited, not revolted. She wanted him to do that, oh, yes, and she clutched the grass with both fists and came violently against his mouth.

Then he slid his body upwards, maddeningly slow, laughing. He kept one knee between her thighs, rubbing her, taunting her. Her breath came in little gasps while she pulled his shirt from his pants and rubbed her breasts frantically against him. Then she freed his erect, straining penis from his pants, bending to touch its tip with her tongue.

Heather felt a moment of confusion. It was cold, cold against her mouth, and why would it be cold? When she had done this for Stan, he was warm and straining against her lips. Why was he cold?

But she forgot the strange feeling that the sensation of his iciness against her lips gave her when he roughly pulled her up and pinned both her arms over her head with one hand. He kissed her mouth, her breasts, and the little hollow in her neck where a pulse beat quickly. He seemed to like that spot the best, returning to it again and again, and Heather writhed sensuously against his mouth as she felt him begin to suckle there. She let her mind and body waft away on the mysterious primitive tide of the feelings he provoked in her. He could do anything he wanted, she would let him do anything that he wanted . . .

It began to hurt a little, that suckling of her neck, and so she tossed her head restlessly. Then he positioned her so that her knees were over his shoulder, her legs dangling down his back. And he thrust inside her, making her scream, but he didn't stop. He ignored her cries and kept driving cruelly into her. Her heels drummed against his back, first with the pain, and then with the pleasure that mounted feverishly as he thrust deeper and deeper within her. She felt herself crest the top of a wave and she was crying out with the pain and the glory of it. She climaxed over and over again.

When he pulled out of her and turned her over roughly, Heather made a dim sound of protest. Then her thrust into her from behind. She felt as if he were tearing her apart; he was fast and brutal, pounding vigorously against her, and Heather squealed with the pain of it. He was too big, too big ... and then his hand slipped between her legs and began to rub knowingly against the moist warmth there, and she forgot her protests. His teeth once again found that spot on her neck, and she moaned as he slapped hard against her buttocks and suckled her throat. And she thought that she screamed as she came once again, but it was only a little whimper, and she felt a gush of warmth flood down her neck. And her life slipped away while Sang Adorer grasped her hips with both hands and pumped furiously upon her.

He left her lying there sprawled on her stomach underneath the orange tree, in the peace of the night that she had always liked the best.

* * *

"I did what you wanted," the rat faced little hotel manager whined. "I never told nobody nothing about the kid."

Leaning back in the hotel manager's own chair and keeping him standing in front of him like a penitent, Sang fingered the gold medallion that hung around his neck and stared at the man. Hard to believe that this bit of offal ran a hotel, and quite efficiently, to hear Dan tell it. And he had been instrumental in the distribution of their little product, too. Of course, part of that had to do with Dan, who so reassured the customers with his nice, normal face. It couldn't be bad for you if this pleasant, wholesome man took it, could it? Of course not.

It amused Sang to keep the man so sweaty and off-balance. So scared, though he could not have said why. The man would have a heart attack if he really knew what kind of danger he was in right now, Sang thought idly. I could rip off his head and drink from it as if it were a goblet. I could crush his bones and drink their jelly. One day when I don't need him anymore, perhaps I will. He smiled coldly, and the man backed off a step with a cry. Sang laughed.

"Well done," he said slowly and laughed again when the man gave an audible sigh of relief. "And did you have official visitors?"

"Some cop came by. His grandma called to bitch me out. And a couple of young girls came by, too. Wanted to know did Dan work here, when was his shift, did I know anything about his social life. I gave them all a little trickle of information, because I figured they'd get suspicious if I didn't tell them anything."

Sang leaned forward and raised one eyebrow slowly.

"Two girls came by?"

"Yeah, one was the blond you told me to watch for. She had some Hispanic chick with her."

"Ah," Sang Adorer said gently, steepling his fingers together and staring intently over the top of them. "And did this chick have a name?"

The skinny man raised a trembling hand to his mouth and wiped away the sweat that beaded there.

"Shannon, I think she called her. Yeah, Shannon, that was it."

Sang Adorer leaned back in the chair once again. "Ah," he said. "Shannon." He smiled. "Shannon."

* * *

Shannon edged around the corner of a house, trying to control her panting. She'd been sound asleep in her bed when something had wakened her. Something had been in her room at home, something that had frightened her. So she'd snuck out in the middle of the night, going right out the window. She couldn't think straight lately, everything was fuzzy all the time. The only time she felt right is when she took the drugs, but they wore off too quickly, and she was taking more and more. And now it didn't seem to be helping her at all. She didn't feel the way she'd felt in the beginning when she took it; she didn't feel god-like and all-powerful now. She just felt scared and out of control. Maybe she shouldn't have left the house; maybe she should have stayed inside. Because whatever had been in her room was chasing her out here now. She couldn't hear it or see it, but she knew it was there. *He'd* sent something after her.

If anyone were close, they would hear her harsh breathing, so she must be silent. She crept silently between the houses, then stood against the side of one, bracing her back against the wall. She let her eyes adjust to the darkness. There was something glowing on the wall across from her, and she strained to see it. What was it?

Eyes.

Two pair of eyes.

She gave a harsh cry of despair as Sang Adorer stepped out of the shadows, and Dan stepped out right behind him. Then the cry turned into a bloodcurdling scream as Sang smiled crookedly at her, his fangs prominent. With a roar, he was upon her. He ripped his fangs into her breast, stabbing her, slashing her, draining her dry . . . and Shannon didn't lose consciousness, not until the very end. She died in agony, and somewhere in the back of her dying mind she thought that maybe it was what she deserved.

And when he had finished with her, she looked like a broken doll that some child had dashed repeatedly against the wall. Her head had been torn completely away from her body. One of her legs lay atop the garbage cans across from her.

But there was no blood spill. There was none left to spill after Sang finished his play.

And there was no time to retrieve the body, because lights were going on everywhere and heads were popping out of doors and windows. Who could have slept through all of that?

Afterward, Dan wondered shakily if he would ever forget her screams at the end. The people at the house, they were stoned when they died, and he'd always made sure that they had a lot of the stuff, not to lessen their pain, but to lessen his work ... and it *had* blunted some of their pain, even if that hadn't been his intention. He knew that Shannon was high when Sang killed her; he could read the signs 'cause he'd seen her high so many times, but her pain hadn't been lessened. Just the opposite, in fact. It had seemed to intensify it. And her cries had echoed down the alley between the houses like the haunted shrieking of the damned.

* * *

Jessie didn't see Shannon at any of classes at school the next day, so Jessie decided to go to Dan Jackson's apartment alone. She wasn't sure that she wanted the other girl along, anyway; she'd been acting so strangely and the vision or whatever that she'd had of the worm in Shannon's heart really freaked her out. It made her feel sick to even touch Shannon now.

For a twenty, the manager of the building where Dan Jackson and his grandmother lived told Jessie that Dan hadn't been at home for at least a week. He knew because the old lady had told him, bitching up a storm about the worthless grandson of hers. For another twenty, he'd told Jessie that the old woman had just left to do her weekly grocery shopping, and wouldn't be back for hours. She did it at the same time every week, and she was too cheap to spring for a taxi or the bus, so she walked home, pushing the cart from the store. And the old bitch never took them back, either. See all those carts abandoned in the parking lot? That was because of her. Seemed like she could take one of them back once in a while, but she never did. When there got to be too many of them, he'd call the grocery store and they would send somebody down here to get them.

For yet more money, he unlocked the door and let her go inside their apartment. Jessie got the distinct feeling that for another twenty he'd have held the old woman down while she hacked her head off with a pocketknife, or did anything to her that she wanted to do. She shuddered at the thought, and made up her mind to hurry up. Maybe Dan Jackson had paid him twenty to call him whenever Jessie showed up. Or maybe he hadn't left the building at all. Maybe he was waiting in here for her.

But her fears were ungrounded. Nobody was there.

Jessie walked slowly down the hallway in the center of the dim apartment. She glanced over at the old woman's bedroom and saw a Bible open in the center of the single bed. The bed was covered with a frayed blanket that had probably once been white, but was now yellowed with age. Everything in the apartment was old, falling apart, decrepit, and not the kind of old that comforts you, the kind of comfort you feel in using things you've owned for years. No one loved the things in this apartment. They merely used them until they were well past using, and then they tossed them away. There was no comfort here in these rooms, only the kind to be found in that Bible, and there probably wasn't much in that. She'd lay money that the old woman was reading strictly from the Old Testament, the kind of stories where a vengeful God was just as likely to smite you down as lift you up.

She walked past a bathroom that was the size of a small closet, with a toilet so close to the other fixtures that you could sit on it and put one foot in the bathtub and the other into the sink without stretching.

She turned into Dan's room. It, too, was as barren as a monk's cell. A single window, too small for even a child to crawl through, let in little light. There was a single bed, a rickety bedside table, and a battered chest of drawers. A plank of wood propped up on concrete blocks held a small collection of paperbacks. Peter Straub's **Koko**, Steven King's **Misery,** and Christopher Pike's **The Cold One** fell up against a few battered old sci-fi titles.

There was nothing else in the room. Nothing personal here, except for the books. Jessie plopped heavily down onto the sagging mattress of the bed, feeling the spring underneath it poke her as she did so. She couldn't imagine spending her childhood in this room. She struggled to kill the sudden compassion that rose in her chest, and let her eyes search the room. What could she tell from this room? Something in here should speak to her, shouldn't it?

What was a killer's room supposed to look like?

She stared at the blank walls and the old furniture with dead eyes, disappointment tasting awful in her mouth. There was nothing here but the kind of poverty that ate your soul and filled you with rage. What in the hell did she think she was doing? There was no way she was going to figure this out on her own. She should just leave it to the cops, like they said.

But they didn't care about Kira and Andy the way that she did. She'd heard the one, that Bennett, talking to the other cop. He'd implied that they weren't looking very hard for the killer. They had been butchered and nobody cared but her. Why was that?

Jessie felt the anger rising up in her. Her fists clenched on the tattered bedspread. It wasn't fair! Someone should care, someone should find the one responsible for these horrible things, and they should be punished. It shouldn't matter that they were taking drugs, and it shouldn't matter about the way that they dressed. They were dead, and they had been murdered.

Her mother's words resonated so clearly in Jessie's mind that she could almost see her face again, the way that cynical little smirk twisted her mobile face and the way one eyebrow rose when she was agitated. She could almost hear the accent bleeding into her mother's voice the way it did whenever she was disturbed. Come to think of it, she could *definitely* hear that down-South, cotton-pickin' twang her mother got whenever she was upset.

"You know why people are mean to kids, don't you, Jess?"

"Because they can be, Mom," Jessie whispered out loud. "Because they can be."

"That's right, baby," her mind-mother said. ***"That's the truth. Power is an aphrodisiac to some. The more you get, the more you want. And an easy way to get it is to make up unreasonable rules and enforce them on people who don't have any power. And that means***

you, kiddo. Some of those people are drawn to jobs where they can have power over children. Teachers. Principals. College Professors. Security Guards. Cops. I know some would say that I'm being paranoid, that this is a bad thing to teach to my child, but it's the truth, girl, and we've all known some of those people. Tell me now, don't you know one or two of those kind right now? They got crappy lives, so they make themselves feel better by stomping all over you. Maybe some of them don't even know why they do it. But you do, now, and knowledge is power, too. Just roll with it. Do what they say, within limits, and think what you want. One day not so long from now, you'll have power of your own."

"I wish it was now, Mom," Jessie said and roughly whisked away a useless tear that leaked unbidden from one eye. "I wish I had power right now."

As she said the words, her fingers tingled as if she'd suddenly stuck them into a light socket. She yelped slightly with the sudden pain, and the springs of the bed squeaked as she moved. Jessie scrubbed her fingers against her jeans, thinking that they'd fallen asleep, but the ache only intensified. Suddenly her twitching hand flopped off of her leg and onto the bed, and the pain diminished. She scraped her fingers experimentally against the coarse cover, and it lessened even more. But something odd was happening. It didn't hurt as much when she slid her hand toward the pillow, but the farther away her hand got from the top of the bed, the more it hurt. Jessie patted her hand around the neatly tucked coverlet, and felt a slight tingle whenever her hand strayed too far toward the foot of the bed. And when she dug her hand underneath the nearly flat pillow and her hand closed around something that crackled, the tingle went away as if it had never been.

Jessie stared down at the paper-wrapped package she held.

"This is some big spooky shit, baby." Mind-Mom said, and the accent wasn't bleeding in now, her voice was all slow Southern sugar. ***"Voodoo***

shit. You need to get up on outta here. Right now, hear me? Something's wrong. Go on, I mean it."

"I hear you," Jessie whispered softly. "I'm gone right now."

And she stuffed the thin package into her jacket pocket and got the hell gone, just like her dead mother had told her to.

CHAPTER SIX

Jessie cupped her trembling hands around the hot chocolate, savoring the warmth. The waitress at the small café she'd darted into had given her a funny look, but she'd waited courteously enough on the sweating, panting, black-clad teenager. Jessie had been running like the devil himself was chasing her, but the exercise hadn't warmed her. She was still cold; way down inside, and the chocolate probably wasn't going to help. It wasn't going to hurt, either, and there was something about the sugared drink that made her feel better. For long minutes, she ignored the package that seemed to be burning a hole in her pocket.

The first thing Jessie pulled out was a printout of an email.

From: danzel1
Date: Tuesday, March 1
To: colt@dl.com, derangedteen@csi.com, delinsk@ilin.com, orangutan@mm.com, usuckyesudo@dl.com, lallomallo@msm.com, sugarcookies@dl.com, livenlovnfool@ex.com
Subject: Stupid parents

I have some bad news I prolly will only be seeing you all over the weekends and Thursday late nights because Im not aloud on the computer anymore from 5 to 9 I hate my parents now cause everyone is on from that time it really pisses me off all they do is use the phone I really need a new line or cable internet or something cause this really sucks. Or I need to get a place of my own, but who can afford that while there going to college? Well cya peeps

Dan

Well, that's weird. Jessie thought. What parents? He lives with his grandmother. And where did he send this from? There's no computer in his house, and they sure don't have the money for one. She looked at the screen names at the top of the email and felt her fingers begin to tremble again.

Sugarcookies was Kira's screen name.

Dan Jackson had computer access there at the Beach Bum. It had been sitting right there at the front desk, and Jessie had seen the icon for AOL on it. What else did that message tell her, except that he couldn't spell? Jessie bent her head down and closed her eyes. She drew in a sharp breath when she finally got it.

This was how he drew them in.

This was how he got his victims. He trolled for them on the internet. He talked to them for weeks and weeks, pretending to be a kid just like them, with regular kinds of problems, and he got to know them by talking online. When they did meet up, he looked younger than he actually was, and he certainly appeared harmless, so the kids weren't alarmed. Then he did what?

She put the email to one side, spread apart the paper wrapping of the package and next pulled two receipts out. Both were from the Silver Unicorn. Jessie wrinkled her nose. The Silver Unicorn was a smoke shop down on the beach, the kind that sold drug paraphernalia masked as tobacco products. And she'd forgotten about it until just now, but it was rumored to sell more than paraphenalia, too. A kid she went to college with had bragged to everyone who would listen that he bought his drugs from the hot Goth chick that worked there, and that she was going to take him to some special Goth party. Then he'd dropped out of the class, and she'd never had to hear any more of his boring lies about all the girls he'd banged, was going to bang, or continued to bang.

The package also contained a picture of a house that looked familiar to Jessie, and a piece of black fabric. She picked up the piece of fabric and felt suddenly sick. It was a square piece of cloth, stiff with some dried substance. Jessie didn't have to bring it to her nose to tell, but she did it anyway, just to make sure.

It reeked of blood.

The cloth had been soaked in blood. She knew it. Jessie closed her eyes and fought off the dizziness she felt. This piece of fabric had been used in some kind of ritual, cut from the clothing of some innocent victim. Then the piece of cloth was soaked in blood ... whose? Andy's? Kira's? Some other poor idiot who didn't know what was going to happen?

Jessie dropped the fabric onto the table and pressed a hand to her eyes. How did she know these things? How did she find the package, come to that? She'd just *understood* somehow that she was going to find something to help her in Dan's room. Something really strange was happening, and she didn't like it. Not at all, at all. Should she give this stuff to Bennett? And if she did, how was she going to explain how she found it? He already thought she had something to do with Andy and Kira's deaths.

She waved the waitress away when she came to ask if Jessie was okay. Her mouth trembled a minute as she stared into the woman's eyes.

"I'm fine," she said numbly. "Just ... fine."

The woman smiled, and Jessie realized all of sudden that she was beautiful. She could see how it was, 40 years ago, when this woman was young and wild. She'd been a babe then, and everyone she met had basked in the light of her gentle eyes. She had a kind heart, and it showed on her face.

"You know, honey," the woman said, "if I were you, I'd go home and talk to my mother. I'd bet money that whatever it is, she can help you with it."

"Yes," Jessie said. "She could."

She paid for her hot chocolate and left a generous tip on the table, not looking at the woman's face again. She didn't want any kindness right now. She'd prefer a little righteous rage.

* * *

When the maid at the hotel opened the door to room 212, she could smell death inside the room.

Juana knew what death smelled like; it had been a frequent visitor to the small town in Mexico where she had grown up. Death wasn't pretty and just some easy fading away, like they showed on the television. Death was ugly and nasty, and it had a stink all of its own. It stank of piss and shit and blood and desperation. And she could smell all of those things in here, in this room.

So she pulled the door shut without looking inside and went down to the front desk to get the manager. He gave her a hard time, but Juana had worked there for a while and she knew how to handle him. She was usually quiet and docile, but she could be stubborn when it was necessary. She merely folded her arms over her chest and repeated again that there was a problem in room 212, and she could not go any further until someone came with her to check it out. He could, of course, have someone else finish her assigned rooms ...

And since the manager was not as big a fool as he sometimes acted and he was short of maids as it was, he mumbled something underneath his breath and came with her. He entered the room and stopped, with Juana right behind him, as soon as he saw what was lying on the beds inside.

A woman in her fifties lay diagonally across the double bed closest to the door, facedown and fully clothed, her head twisted at an impossible angle on her slim neck. One arm was outstretched and a small pistol lay underneath her hand upon the floor. There was no wound visible upon her that they could see; and neither Juana nor the manager made any effort to move closer to take a better look.

Her husband lay on the next bed, rigid, still clothed. He was face-up, with an expression of terror so vivid upon his features that Juana crossed herself and breathed a prayer.

His throat had been torn out. It looked as if an animal had savagely ripped apart the tender flesh of his neck.

But there was no blood.

"*Madre de Dios*," Juana said.

"You can say that again," said the manager. "Fuck."

* * *

Sergeant John Bennett was forty-three and felt every day of it. He looked it today; too many nights without enough sleep and too much stress had caught up with him, and his face looked as gray and rumpled as the suit that he wore. He was tall, well over six feet and solid in a way that made him look heavy until you noticed the muscles straining beneath his clothing. The collar of his white shirt was unbuttoned, his tie pulled down, and his sleeves rolled halfway up his brawny, hairy forearms. He had large, irregular features and thick dark hair that was just going silver. His eyes were a startling green underneath the thick shelf of his brow.

He leveled those eyes at the hotel manager now.

"And nobody reported hearing anything suspicious coming from this room the night before? No fights, no loud noises, nothing?"

"No," the man said again. "There's nothing on the log, and all complaints are supposed to be written down. I got a call in to the night manager, and he should be in soon to talk to you. It had to be last night that it happened, too, because I saw both of them myself right before I left work yesterday. That was about six o'clock. They were just going out to dinner, and they asked me if I knew where they could find good seafood."

John Bennett rubbed his forehead, right above the spot where a headache pounded fiercely, and sighed.

"All right," he said. "We got all that we need from you. We're going to need this room for a while, and we'll let you know when you can start using it again. Might be a couple of days."

"Yeah, right," the manager said. He reminded John of a little banty rooster, strutting back and forth and making a lot of noise. "Like we're going to need it. We sure aren't going to have a rush of customers now after a double murder in one of our rooms. Business is bad enough this year, and now we got cops hanging around all the time and crime scene tape everywhere." And he shook his head and went muttering back to his office.

John sighed again.

"Hey, John," one of the technicians called. "We're done with the photographs, and we're going to flip her over now. Want to come and see?"

But John knew what they were going to find before he even returned to where the woman's body lay. Her throat was going to look just like her husband's did. And he knew that a lot of her blood was going to be missing. Just like he knew that the gun hadn't been fired. Just like he knew that no one at the hotel had heard anything. The violence in this town was escalating beyond belief; each day it seemed that there was a new murder to deal with. Something had to be done, and he didn't know how to do it, or even *whom* to do it to. John Bennett felt helpless, and that was not an emotion that he was comfortable feeling. He was the police; he was in control; but not this time.

They were dealing with a shadow man.

Or a demon.

* * *

The Silver Unicorn was five blocks from downtown, and there was only a light crowd, as Jessie had expected. It was a Wednesday afternoon, and what traffic there was in the smoke shop was clustered at the counter at the other end of the place. They were all guys and they were all leaning on the counter, flirting with the woman who worked there.

Jessie pretended to be interested in a display of pipes, staring fixedly at them in the glass case, but she was really staring at the woman's reflection in the glass. The clerk gestured theatrically and often, her full black sleeves flowing around her as she did so. She also laughed a lot and touched them all frequently, looking brazenly at them with the sloe eyes she had outlined boldly with kohl. She wore large hammered silver earrings and a matching necklace flat against the bronze, smooth skin she displayed so much of with her low-cut silk blouse. She wore a skirt that just barely covered her butt, and she couldn't have been wearing much in the way of underclothing. It would have showed through the thin cloth, and there were no lines marring the lush contours of her figure.

That's what my mom always called a one-inch skirt, Jessie thought sourly. *Because when you wore one of them, you were one inch away from disaster at any given moment. Hate to see what would happen if she ever dropped anything around here. Probably be a riot.*

She wondered how they got away with selling this stuff. These weren't pipes for tobacco; they were used for pot and crack. And those were bongs over there; how could it be legal to sell stuff to use drugs when the drugs themselves were illegal? Not that pot should be illegal anyway. It wasn't any worse than alcohol in her mind. She'd talked about it once with her mom, and had been surprised to find that she had much the same views. Harder drugs were different, but marijuana? How many people did you know who smoked a little weed on Friday nights and then got mad and shot somebody? Too bad you couldn't say the same thing about alcohol.

"Can I help you with something?"

Jessie jerked at the sound of the voice, too intent on her musings to notice that the clerk had approached her end of the counter. She swung her head up to meet the woman's amused gaze. Jessie flushed.

"I'm looking for something," she said carefully, but her voice still cracked a little. "Something that you don't have in the case." She cleared her throat and stared hard at the woman, who flung her hair over her shoulder and looked scornful.

"And what could that be?" she asked coolly.

"Dan Jackson told me I could get it here," Jessie said, and the superior attitude melted away from the clerk as if it had never been.

"Sure," she said, smiling. "If Dan sent you, that's okay then. I'm closing up in about fifteen minutes. Wait outside for me. Oh, I'm Sylvia."

"I'll be in the red Toyota in the parking lot across from the store," Jessie told her, deliberately not giving her own name.

But just then, one of the guys at the counter looked over and waved. Jessie caught the motion from the corner of her eye, and she turned to look. Her heart sank, and she felt like cursing. It was David; she had a math class with him. What a time to run into somebody she knew.

"Hey, Jessie," he called, smiling and happy to see her. "I didn't know you came in here. How are you?"

"Just fine," Jessie said. "Well, see ya tomorrow in class," she called, and turned to leave.

Something had changed in Sylvia's face, but Jessie couldn't tell what it was. Something roiled below the surface of Sylvia's placid expression. Jessie studied her intently, but she couldn't tell what it was. And quite frankly, she didn't want to know. She didn't want to have any more of those visions or whatever they were; she didn't want to see any more little black things wriggling around inside of people.

"I'll wait for you in the car," she said uncertainly. "Red Toyota."

"Fifteen minutes," Sylvia promised. "Just wait for me there."

It was hot in the car, so Jessie started it up and turned on the air conditioner. She didn't see how people in Florida ever survived without air conditioning. She certainly couldn't have. Her car was facing away from the shop, but she could glance in the rearview mirror every once in a while to see when Sylvia came out. And she was the only red car in the lot, so there was no way the girl could miss her. So there wasn't any reason why she couldn't crank the music, was there? Jessie tuned the station to one she liked and was just starting to get into it what they were playing when *wham!* something slammed into her car. Jessie jumped and looked around. What the hell was that?

Boom! The noise this time was louder this time, and immediately in front of her there was a gaping hole in her windshield. Shattered glass went everywhere. While she stared, more glass fell out onto the pavement with a tinkling sound. Jessie gawked at it for a moment before she knew what was going on.

Somebody was shooting at her!

She ducked down, reached for the door handle, and struggled to undo her seatbelt without lifting her head. At that moment a third bullet slammed into the car and punched a hole in the roof. She scrambled out the door and crouched on the ground. God, god, what was she going to do? Bullets could pass through cars easily, no matter what crap you saw on TV about people always hiding behind them. They were only good for cover, not protection. A bullet could easily come through the car and still have enough force to kill her.

Jessie duckwalked around to the front of the car, and then she heard the sound of a car driving fast down the street. She dared to lift her head, and saw a blue Chevy squealing away, with the driver's face turned toward her. Her features were contorted with hate and fear, and she was screaming something unrecognizable out her open window, but Jessie had no problem recognizing her.

It was Sylvia, from the Silver Unicorn.

Jessie stood up slowly and looked at the damage to her car, feeling sick. There was absolutely no way that she was going to be able to keep this incident from Mrs. Davis. And she was going to have to report it to the police, too.

She wondered if her car insurance covered bullet holes.

She called Mrs. Davis on her cell phone and told her that she had been shopping for a gift for a friend's birthday, and that when she came back to her car, it had three bullet holes in it. In minutes, Mrs. Davis had her insurance agent and a police officer there. The cop seemed a little skeptical of her story, but he took her explanation as stated, and the insurance agent got the car towed and gave her a ride home. He left her at her front door with a promise of a check for repairs to the car the very next day. It all worked out.

But Jessie had a problem getting to sleep that night. She was in over her head, and she knew it.

* * *

Sometimes, when Christina Brown felt irritable and restless, she'd go for a drive.

Sometimes when the kids just got to be too much, and her husband was driving her crazy, she'd pick up the car keys out of the basket in the foyer and head on out the door. Ron knew better than to complain. She wasn't going out drinking, or meeting some man; Christina just liked to drive around. She fantasized sometimes about just keeping on going, but that was just a fantasy she used as a stress reliever. She loved Ron and the kids, she really did, and she'd never leave them. But it was nice just to cruise around in her nice air-conditioned car, playing the radio at top volume and singing along. She could *pretend* that she didn't have a husband or any children at home.

That was usually enough to make her feel better, and she'd come home cheerfully enough, kiss Ron on his forehead, and look with pride on the children as they slept curled up in their beds like the little angels that they certainly weren't.

Tonight, a harvest moon hung low in the sky, colored a brilliant orange by the dying embers of the sun. Christina caught her breath at the beauty of it, and drove slowly down the bumpy road. Usually, she drove around in the part of town down by the mall, but tonight she hadn't felt like seeing any people, so she'd driven down to McGregor and then turned toward the river to try and find a road down there. And sure enough, she'd found one; a bumpy dirt road with huge holes that nearly engulfed her little Mazda when she drove through them. Thank God it wasn't raining; her car would sink in those holes and they'd never find her again.

It was dark back here; she didn't want to run over anything, so Christina kept her speed down. She decided all at once that she wanted to walk; usually when she did this night driving, she stayed in the car, but that moon was calling to her. And it wasn't as hot and sticky tonight as it usually was, so she'd just park her car as far out of the road as she could get it in case someone else drove down this way, and take a little hike.

She could hear the distant sounds of the city when she got out of the car, but mostly what she heard was the sounds of the wild; the rustle of small animals in the bushes, the sough of the wind through the trees, the far away sound of water upon the shore. She loved the sound of the water, the hiss and suck of the tide, the sparkle of the moonlight on the moving water. She even liked the fecund *smell* of the water; it appealed to some primitive part of her psyche.

She took a narrow path through the woods, searching out the sound of that water she knew was close. She could smell the loam of the earth all around her, and she breathed it in deeply. Christina could feel the stress melting away from her body, could feel herself grow more tranquil with every step that she took.

She practically skipped down a little slope down toward the river. The moonlight reflected brilliantly off the shifting water, and Christina smiled. She stood for a long time and watched the rhythm of it, as the water bent and swayed and fell and rose again.

She noticed a movement out of the corner of her eye and turned sharply. A figure seemed to scuttle out of sight, and was that a giggle that she heard? Suddenly Christina became frightened of the very dark that had so sustained her only moments ago. She didn't hesitate; she started for her car at a dead run. Christina was on the track team in high school, and she was still in pretty good shape; she could still run like the wind. Behind her she heard cursing and loud noises as someone thrashed through the bushes after her, and she didn't slow down until she reached her car.

At that moment, if ghosts and goblins and witches had jumped out at her from behind her innocuous little Mazda, she wouldn't have been surprised. This night seemed malevolent. In the night, strange things could happen. That was the time when you believed. During the daytime, you scoffed, because when the sun shone brightly and everything seemed sane, it was easy to dismiss your fears.

And when Christina started for home, her hands shaking from the adrenaline and the fear that coursed through her body, she swore grimly to herself that she would only drive around from now on when she went out at night. Not get out of the car. Not ever.

Because somewhere deep inside of her, she knew. There really were monsters out there, and they had been going to eat her up. And she was lucky to be alive.

CHAPTER SEVEN

Taylor Cameron was seventeen, and she thought that Florida was paradise. She'd come to this place two years ago now, and it was so warm here that she could sleep in the park nearly year-round. There were only a couple of nights a year that it got so cold she had to take shelter indoors, and there were plenty of places to do that. She bathed in the fountain at night, she panhandled or worked some little shit job during the day, or if she decided to, she'd just head on down to the beach. She was pretty and built nice and she knew it, so she'd lounge around in her bikini and wiggle her butt a little whenever anyone interesting walked by. She could always find some fine young man to buy her lunch. And sometimes she got to stay for a day or two in some nice hotel room, sleeping in their nice bed, taking hot showers and never having to clean up after herself. Once she got lucky and got to stay for two whole weeks before the guy had to go home. He tried to get her to go with him, but Taylor wasn't about to trade Florida for Minnesota. He was trippin' and she told him so.

She'd been born and raised in southern Illinois, and there couldn't have been any two places more different. She was fond of saying that there were three things they grew in her hometown, and she didn't care for any of them: Corn, cow shit, and rednecks.

She'd been miserable in her hometown. Her daddy was drunk all the time, and his favorite sport when he was drinking was to beat on her and her momma. Her momma didn't do anything about it but go to church and cry. But Taylor didn't go to church, and she'd stopped crying a long time ago. She noticed that God hadn't been anywhere to be seen when her daddy had broke her arm by throwing her out of a moving car. And God sure didn't seem to care that everybody in that one-horse town thought she was trash just for being related to that disgusting old man.

So she'd run away, soon as she was big enough to hitch a ride out of town. She'd kissed that place and all those idiots goodbye when she was thirteen, and she was never, ever going to clap eyes on it again.

She'd hung out in Atlanta for a while, until she got word that some skinny, mean little guy name of Cujo wanted her to join his little group of girls. He wanted to farm her out, put her on the street peddling her ass full time, but she wasn't no prostitute. She was just a girl doing what she had to do to get by, and she'd seen what happened to those others after a while. They smoked crack so they could stand to do what they did, and then the crack took over and they sold themselves so they could pay for crack. She was too smart for that shit. She hadn't left one prison so she could be locked up in another.

Taylor had hauled ass out of Atlanta in a hurry, before that dude Cujo could find her and force her to work for him. A sweet little old truck driver had taken her all the way to Fort Myers, Florida, and she'd never left. She was never going to leave either. She had it made here.

She was dozing now by the low wall that bordered the park where she liked to sleep when something woke her. It was her favorite place to sleep outside; she rolled herself up in a little blanket on the soft grass, and it was as fine a bed as she'd ever had growing up.

Taylor was groggy when she first woke, and she was slightly chilled. She didn't know why she was awake, so she lay still and listened carefully. You could never be too careful when you were alone. It was only her sharp wits and her good instincts that had saved her butt many a time.

She heard church bells somewhere toll the hour; it was midnight. That must have been what woke her, though it didn't, usually. She'd got used to it.

Little by little, uneasiness began to creep over her. Though ordinarily she liked it that way, tonight it seemed too dark and so eerie in the park.

The wind had picked up, and it swirled incessantly around her and moaned like some disembodied spirit. It died down for a moment, and the utter stillness somehow seemed worse.

Taylor began to wish that she'd found a sweet little boy on the beach today. Then she'd be sleeping in some soft bed instead of being scared to death in the park that she usually loved. She glanced around fearfully. In the dark and afraid, trees became gnarled shadows creeping up on her, signs became ghosts rising out of the ground. She was suddenly on the verge of hysteria, shivering heavily.

"Now what's the matter with you, girl?" she said out loud, shakily, to herself. "Ain't nothing here that ain't always here. Calm down."

But it didn't help.

And she heard a sound on the other side of the wall. And Taylor got the feeling that something, someone, was on the other side of the wall, just waiting for her. She felt the hair rising on the back of her neck. Every nerve in her body told her she wasn't being foolish, but she tried to convince herself so. She held her breath, and heard nothing. Then she let it out with a little gasp, and then she strained her ears and held her breath to listen once more. And Taylor became convinced that when she held her breath, that the *something* that was over there was being still and listening to her.

There was a scraping sound on the other side of the wall, directly across from her.

"Who is it?" she cried sharply. "Who's there?"

Her eyes flew up to the wall, but she felt paralyzed. She couldn't tear herself away, or run, as she wanted to. She was hypnotized as if in a nightmare, rooted to the spot with her head thrown back and her eyes staring overhead.

Through the gloom of the night, she finally saw him. She opened her mouth and let out an ululating cry of terror that was nearly the last sound she ever made.

And her last thought before he forced himself inside her struggling body, laughing, and all her lifeblood slipped down his evil throat was that she had been right. She was never, ever going to clap eyes on Southern Illinois again.

He kept her alive for a long time, playing with her.

* * *

John Bennett lay in wait for the other cop like a Florida panther waited for prey in the swamps, his anger and impatience contained only by his strong will. He sat in the chair in the kitchen, watching the clock. 2:40.

When he heard the rattle of keys in the lock, he slipped silently behind the door and he waited. When the door swung shut, he spoke.

"You lied to me, Corey," he said, and the young cop bolted toward the back door with a scream of panic. Bennett grabbed him and slung him into the wall, using the man's own impetus against him.

"That wasn't very nice, now was it?" Bennett asked grimly when he'd subdued him. He knelt on his back as he forced the cuffs on him. Then he yanked him up viciously. "You weren't thinking of leaving, were you? You weren't going to get very far, anyway, because there's two other cops outside."

"I don't know what you're talking about!" Corey blubbered, spittle collecting at the corners of his mouth. Bennett could tell by his eyes that he was high, still flying. He smelled of sweat and fear.

Bennett shook him, not caring that Corey's head banged a time or two against the wall. "Don't lie anymore," he said softly. "I'm tired of finding bodies. There seems to be a disproportionate number of female victims, Corey. I got four girls of my own, and that fact is making me very uncomfortable. I don't want to look at one more dead woman. Talk, and tell me the truth, because I'm not very patient, and I'm feeling a little violent tonight. That's not a good combination, now is it, Corey? These people are escalating, Corey, and if you've got any brain cells left after burning them up with all the shit you've been putting in your body, you'll talk. I got at least ten dead in the past two weeks, and they're all missing major amounts of blood. And I might have been a little closer to figuring it out if you hadn't been obstructing the investigation the whole time. You told me that you ran Dan Jackson through the computer and he came up clean, but that's not true, is it now? I did a little checking on my own, and he's not exactly Snow White. And you two are cozy little friends, aren't you? I know that he called you earlier tonight, right before you went out."

"Yeah, we got a tap on your phone," he said when Corey's head jerked up. "I suspected you days ago and got a warrant. Got one to search here, too, and we found your little stash. Found a bunch of money, and a bunch of drugs, too, Corey. You been dealing, huh? Where's Dan? Where are the rest of your psycho friends hiding out?"

Corey felt a pounding in his head, and a wave of shaking weakness spread over him. He leaned over and retched, a hand pressed to his burning stomach. It had all gone wrong, so very very wrong. He'd screwed himself into a deep hole that he was never going to get out of. Corey could hear Sergeant Bennett begin swearing when he didn't answer and began to cry into his hands instead. It was the drugs, just the drugs, he wasn't a killer, he wasn't. He never would have done it if it hadn't been for the meth. It was the meth. Not him. The meth.

* * *

The pounding on the door brought her halfway down the stairs, but Mrs. Davis got to the door first, and Jessie stopped and waited to see who it was. Sergeant Bennett stepped into the house, lean and grim, eyes dark. She recognized that look; the look they all got when they came to the house to tell you. The look that the cop had when he came to tell her about her mother. The bearer of bad tidings. The bringer of death. She saw the color drain from Mrs. Davis' face, the stricken look in her eyes. Together they turned to look at her, and she demanded to know what it was, what had happened now. He told her, and the knowledge pierced her like a stiletto through the heart.

Shannon was dead.

She could see their lips still moving, but she couldn't hear them. She couldn't hear anything above the pounding of her pulse, and that awful screaming noise that was coming from somewhere. She put her hands to her ears. She wished it would stop, she wished it would stop! And then she realized that it was her, that she was the one making that awful noise.

Because Shannon was dead.

"No!" she screamed, stumbling down the last few stairs. She struck Bennett's chest with her fists, over and over. This couldn't be happening. This couldn't be real, because nobody should have to lose all the people that they cared about in the space of six months. God couldn't be that cruel. It was just a bad dream; just another dream was all.

Jessie sank down to the floor, dazed and weak, dimly hearing Mrs. Davis cry raggedly above her. And when Sergeant John Bennett crouched down beside her and his strong arms encircled her, she clutched at them with all her strength. Because she had to hold onto something. She had to have something to hold onto, didn't she? Because all the people who had defined her world were gone. She was alone, her whole world had turned upside down, and nobody could blame her for holding on tight, could they? Could they?

And the tears that she had fought for so long soaked into his shirt. John Bennett held her close, whispering softly to her, brushing his lips against her hair. She had been so brave through this whole thing, such a fighter ... and she was so young. Now it was time to let go of the pain she had held for so long. And he helped her let it go, cradling her in his arms as if she were one of his own daughters; soothing her pain because he knew that he had so often missed soothing theirs.

The kitchen was where Mrs. Davis always took her serious discussions. When Jessie's grades had started to drop after her mother's death, this was where they had talked about it. When she suggested that Jessie might like to see a psychologist to help her deal with her grief and anger, it had been from the kitchen that she suggested it. The cheery room with its bright white walls, pictures of fruit, and bright yellow curtains was the place Mrs. Davis felt most comfortable, and that was where she took them now. She refused to allow anyone to speak until they all had a drink and a snack. And she watched Jessie like a hawk until she took a nibble of the brownie she'd been given. Then she took the necklace from around her neck and handed the gold cross on the delicate chain to Jessie.

"I had a dream last night, dear," she said quietly. "And in it your mother told me to give you this. And though I could ignore it, I've always felt that dreams can mean something. So I'd feel better if you took this and kept it with you."

Jessie stared at it for a moment, then put the cross around her neck. Sergeant Davis, who sat sprawled in the chair opposite Jessie and had been quiet up to this point, cleared his throat. He told her about the policeman who had been involved in the trade of methamphetamines. They suspected he knew much more about the murder of Shannon Alonzo than he was saying. He'd been arrested, but he wasn't talking.

Jessie looked at him in dawning comprehension. "So you really were trying to find the killer? You did care? Because I heard you tell that other cop that nobody cared about drug addicts getting killed."

"You heard that?" he asked, flushing. "Yeah, I said that to him. I tried to make him think that I wasn't looking very hard for the killer. We already suspected him by then and we were working on a warrant to get a tap on his phone." He smiled crookedly at her, and Jessie forgave him, just a little, and then the smiled dropped away from his face and the customary frown came back.

"And when we searched his room, we found a scrap of paper with your name and address on it, Jessie. I'm going to share some things I know about this case with you, Jessie, and I want you to share what you know with me. I don't think that you're involved, but I think that you know something that these people think that you shouldn't. That information could help me bring in everybody who is involved in this."

"About six or seven months ago, a dealer named Ricky Blake got killed. Gunshot to the head. He specialized in crank, Ricky did, but he'd sell other stuff sometimes, too. Had a couple of witnesses who walked in on the whole thing, but they were looking to buy from Ricky and they were high already. All they could give us is that it was a big guy, young, with blond hair. But he left his gun."

Bennett leaned back in the chair and the legs creaked with the motion. "Only that gun was supposed to be locked in the evidence room at the police station. It had been used in a robbery a year ago. And that meant it was a cop. We put together everything we had from the killing and the witnesses. We eliminated all the cops who were on duty when the killing took place. We crossed off all the women and the men over forty. We got it down to two guys who had access to the evidence room who fit the profile, and Corey was one of them. Turns out the other guy was at his mother's funeral in Boise, Idaho that day, and there were dozens of witnesses. That left Corey. We got one of the dealers from the tap on his phone. Do you know a Dan Jackson?"

"I think I've got some stuff in my room that you might be interested in," Jessie said slowly, guiltily. And she went to get the package of things she'd taken from Dan Jackson's bedroom. And then she'd told them everything that had been happening to her. She felt better now that someone else knew about Sylvia shooting at her, and she'd told Sergeant Bennett about the threatening phone call and about the night somebody broke into the house while Mrs. Davis was gone. And even about the midnight visit she'd got from the man that she suspected was Sang Adorer. But Jessie left out the part about her dead mother talking to her and what Shannon had said about real vampires, or about the strange vision that she'd had. She was not an idiot. She didn't want them locking her up in the loony bin somewhere, after all.

Later, in her room, Jessie sat on her bed thinking about the picture she had found in Dan Jackson's room. Sergeant Bennett had read her the riot act about getting involved and for withholding information from the police. He'd told her that he could actually put her in jail for what she'd done, even though she'd done it for the right reasons. He'd also said that he'd put her in protective custody right now if it weren't for the fact that they'd already begun arresting some of the people they suspected were the killers. He felt that the danger to her wasn't as severe now, but it had been then. But he'd still had a police officer come over here to spend the night, and they were going to have a guard around for a few days. Sergeant Bennett had been really upset, and Mrs. Davis had, too. She could have been killed just like her friends, they'd both told her.

Jessie sighed. She had to do something to keep from going crazy. She didn't want to think about everybody being dead. She just had to block it out right now. So she'd think about all the stuff that she'd found out, instead. Keep her brain busy, so that she wouldn't have time to wonder about the torment that Kira and Andy and Shannon must have gone through before they died.

And her mother ...

Stop it! she ordered herself sharply. Just stop it right now. She willed the tears away and began to think.

Jessie closed her eyes and summoned up the picture of the house that was printed on her brain. She knew this house from somewhere. She just had to remember where it was. She thought and thought about all the stuff until her eyes were burning and her head was swimming. She'd call Sergeant Bennett tomorrow and talk to him about it. He wasn't so bad, maybe. At least he cared about finding the person who killed Shannon and Kira.

She had to get some sleep. Jessie fell across the bed, yawning, and was asleep almost immediately. And while she was sleeping, as often happens, the answer came to her.

They were ten, and the three of them were supposed to be staying with Shannon's Abuela while their mothers worked at the Saturday job they'd found, but Abuela, as they all called her, the mother of Shannon's mother, was old. She'd fallen asleep, and the girls knew it was the perfect time to go exploring. Abuela's house was down by the river, and Jessie had heard her mother and Shannon's talking about it long ago. Abuela's husband had bought the land and built the house years and years ago, when the land was cheaper. Then, it had been a small Cuban community within Fort Myers. But all her neighbors had sold out and moved away, one by one, and now sprawling, colossal monstrosities peopled with young white professionals surrounded the tiny little Cuban woman in her tiny little house. Shannon's Abuela felt out of place in her own neighborhood, but her husband had made this house with his own hands and she couldn't leave. All her memories were here.

They turned off of the path that wound down from the house and wandered idly along the riverbank. Kira picked up a stick and swished it back and forth in the water, splashing the other two. Laughing, they retaliated and when they were done, they were all wet from head to toe. But that was okay; the Florida sun was hot, and they'd dry quickly.

"Come on, let's do it," Shannon urged, wringing the water out of the long braid that her mother always made of her thick, dark hair. "We won't get caught. Nobody ever comes here."

"Yes," Kira said. "I want to do it, too. We always say we're going to, but we never do."

They were talking about going into the house.

For as long as they could remember, they'd been fascinated by the abandoned house down by the river that they'd found. When they'd told Shannon's Abuela about it, she'd warned them away. It was an evil house, she insisted, and there was bad *gris gris* there. Shannon had laughed scornfully behind her back, telling them not to pay attention. She was just an ignorant old peasant woman, and she was superstitious. Everyone knew that those things were just made up stories.

Always before, they'd started to go inside but had eventually lost their nerve and turned away. Something about the huge, looming place made Jessie uneasy, and she listed her fears out loud to the other two.

The flooring might be rotten. There might be pygmy rattlers in there. Or coral snakes. Or palmetto bugs, those giant flying cockroaches that she thought were a sick joke from God. Or rats. Or monsters ...

Kira and Shannon jeered, but Jessie still hesitated. It wasn't that she didn't like to take risks. There was nothing she liked more than going off and exploring, poking along the banks of the Caloosahatchee, skipping stones into the water. Sometimes she would lose her footing and fall into the warm water, but falling into the water couldn't kill her.

Going into abandoned houses could.

"Come on!" Shannon said impatiently once again. "If you don't go with us, we're going alone."

"Yes, come with us," Kira said with a sly smile. "My Jessie wouldn't be afraid."

They all laughed, because that was what Kira's sister Caitlin had called Jessie when she learned to talk. My Jessie. Jessie had played with her a lot because she was enthralled with the sweet-smelling little monster, and Caitlin followed her around like a little puppy. Kira had taken the term for a while to tease, and now used it whenever she wanted to cajole Jessie into doing something. So Jessie said yes, but a small shudder worked its way up her spine. She didn't want to do it, but she didn't want them to call her a chicken, either.

In the back of the house was a small door, covered over with weathered boards that had long since shrunk with age. Through the gaps between the boards she could make out the door itself, held closed by a padlock on a rusted hasp.

Gingerly, they tested one of the boards, and the corroded nails gave way with a screeching groan. It took them only scant seconds to pull three more off, making a hole big enough to climb through. Shannon grabbed the padlock and Jessie held her breath. If the padlock gave, she would be committed to going inside.

"Hold on, hold on," she thought. "Be stuck. Be stuck."

But the rusted hasp broke loose, leaving the lock in Shannon's hand. She discarded it onto the ground with a moue of distaste. Kira pushed the door open and crawled through the opening, Shannon pushing impatiently behind her. Jessie was the last to squirm through the gap. For a moment, the deep shadows blinded her, but then her eyes adjusted to the dim light of the interior. She looked around. They were standing inside something that obviously used to be a kitchen. The remains of an old cook stove were shoved off to one corner of the room. A sink hung crookedly from the wall, drooping almost to the floor. It all made Jessie feel very uneasy inside. She didn't know why, but there was something wrong here, something very wrong . . .

Shannon pushed on the swinging door that led into a hallway, and it gave with a creak. They walked down the hall silently, looking at the peeling wallpaper, passing a huge staircase, until they arrived at a large central room. Kira suddenly exclaimed in wonder. There were paintings still hanging on these walls. Beautiful paintings, exquisitely rendered in vivid colors. There must have been at least fifteen of them, and Jessie could tell even at the age of ten that they shouldn't have been left in an abandoned house. These were good paintings, perhaps even great ones, and they would be worth a lot of money.

But Jessie felt queasy when she looked at them, and she wouldn't let Kira take one off the wall and carry it home the way that she wanted to. Because there was blood in every painting. Jessie whirled to look at them all, feeling sicker and sicker. A fox was being torn to pieces by hounds in one. In another, a dead bird lay upon a table, dripping crimson onto the floor. A deer was being set upon by wolves, and it was still alive, still trying to struggle to its feet while the carnivorous, rapacious canines ate great, dripping chunks out of its flesh. A man in a loincloth was being hacked to death by warriors in armor, his mouth leaking blood and his eyes full of agony.

They were all full of blood. And Jessie suddenly realized what else was bothering her about the house. There wasn't any dust.

If this house had been standing vacant for all these years, where was the dirt? Where were the bird nests, and the insect life that naturally accumulated in places like these?

Why wasn't it dirty in here?

There was another hallway that led off from the room and led in the opposite direction to the back of the house. Shannon wanted to go down it, but Jessie threw a fit and refused to go any further.

Because the house looked empty, but it didn't feel empty. It felt as if something or someone was lurking inside these walls, waiting for them to come closer. *And it was down that other hallway, and it would kill them and play in their blood, and it would be just like those horrible pictures.* The house was whispering to them, wanting them, and Jessie wondered if there had ever been other visitors to this house. And if the visitors had found what was waiting here for them, and if they'd screamed in agony but no one had heard them. And Jessie knew that they had to leave now, before it was too late. Before whatever it was came out of its room and got them. She whimpered and moved closer to the others.

"Let's go," she said urgently. "*There's something wrong here.*"

A sudden loud noise made them all scream out in panic, run down the hallway and back out the way that they had come, their hearts pounding in fright. Once outside, they looked at each other and laughed, because it all seemed so silly now. Shannon pushed Jessie and called her scaredycat. Kira said boastfully that she hadn't been afraid, she just didn't want to make Shannon and Jessie feel bad 'cause they were the only ones running.

But Shannon and Kira must have felt the same things that Jessie had felt in that house, because they never went back into it again. They never even discussed it. When Abuela died a few years later, the family sold the house and the land it stood on and divided the money.

And in Jessie's troubled sleep, she was again standing at the back door to that house. And she knew that she must enter it, once again.

She put her hand on the doorknob, and she felt its coldness travel all the way to the center of her heart. She turned the knob and went inside. The door opened soundlessly, just as she remembered.

It was as quiet as a tomb inside the house.

She had left the outside world behind and stepped into an ancient one, a world so different and frightening that it made her feel as if her blood had turned to ice in her veins. It pumped sluggishly through her, and Jessie moved slowly, slowly down the hallway. She was in the center room once again. Shadows danced all around her, and a glow seeped from underneath a door that seemed so far away. The door at the end of the other hallway. That hallway that had frightened her when she was a child; the hallway that frightened her now.

And a voice called her name.

"Jessie," it said, sweetly, seductively. "Come to me, Jessie. Come to me now."

She knew that voice. It was the voice of the man who had tried to force his way into her house.

It was the voice of the man who thought he was a vampire. It was the voice of Sang Adorer.

Jessie saw the paintings all around her, still filled with bold reds and greens and blues. The paintings should not still be so bright, so filled with vivid color; they should have been dulled and dirty, but something in this place kept them fresh. Huge war-horses trampled fallen men in them; there were broken bodies and decapitated heads and men bound by chains and dragged behind horses. And in all the scenes of slaughter, the blood gleamed bright scarlet, seeming almost to ooze from the frames.

Blood and death was all around her.

And Sang Adorer called her name, over and over. She stepped forward into the darkness, the noise of her footsteps echoing in the house.

She opened the door to the room, and Sang Adorer stood there in the empty room, in all of his beauty. He held out a hand to her; he seemed kind and benevolent, and he smiled at her. Jessie started to smile back, then stopped. She squinted her eyes. There was something wrong here, something ... Jessie stared hard at the man dressed all in black. She did what Grandma Belle had told her to do, and looked with the eyes underneath her eyes.

Jessie looked deep beneath the surface beauty, behind his gilded skin. She saw a glint of something that exuded evil, and if she squinted, she could see it. Jessie concentrated harder, staring hard, ignoring his voice that spoke so gently and harmoniously.

And then she saw, clearly; Sang Adorer's very bones were black with rot. While she concentrated, she watched his face change. It melted in front of her like it was made of wax, and she could see the entire evil underneath. His teeth lengthened and became fangs, and his eyes were red glowing circles of pure, scorching hate that wanted to eat her whole.

This was the true face of Sang Adorer she was seeing. He was a demon.

"I'm your friend," the monster-face said to her, and it made Jessie sick to hear that honeyed, melodious voice coming from that face of evil.

"Use your true voice," she said. "I know what you are."

Jessie realized that the room had changed, too. It was no longer empty; an altar made of some dark stone lay directly Sang Adorer. And Jessie shuddered when she saw the dark stains upon the altar, because she knew that the stains were from blood. The blood of all those that he had killed.

And now she began to see other things appear inside the once empty room. There was a broken skull, grinning up at her. The bones of thighs, and hands, and ribs lay intertwined in the terrible room. And as

Jessie watched in horror, more and more bones began to appear, skulls and feet and spines, until the room began to fill. And when the bones had filled the room, the skeletons began to stack on top of each other, rising higher and higher between the two of them; the pile was up to Sang Adorer's waist now, and he took a step back and hissed in rage.

"What is this?" he hissed. "Who dares to interfere with me?"

"***Piss off***," said a too-familiar voice, and Jessie laughed. She'd never known anyone except her mother to use that expression.

"***It's time to go, baby***," her mother said. "***Go on home now. You know what he is, and that's the most important thing. He'll never fool you again. He's evil lurking behind a pretty illusion, and you can see that now.***"

A hand seemed to caress her face, and Jessie smiled at the feeling.

"You were never alone," her mother's voice said in her ear. ***"I was always here. When the undead called you, I sent you the memory of the house so that you would remember how you felt inside it that first time. And I was right beside you, Jessie, the whole time. Every step you took in that place of evil, I took, too."***

"I don't believe in this, Mom," Jessie said, and there were tears in her voice. "I don't believe in vampires and demons and the undead. I don't believe in any of this. I don't even believe in *you*. You're dead, and I'm only dreaming."

"Oh, honey," said her mother's voice. ***"It's more like a nightmare, isn't it?"***

Jessie woke with a start. The house in the picture. The house that he had called her to. It was the abandoned house down by the river, the one that Abuela used to warn them away from. The one that she said was full of bad magic.

And as scared as she was, Jessie knew what she had to do. She had to go back to that house.

CHAPTER EIGHT

It was easy to sneak away from the cop downstairs. He was looking for someone to try and break in, not break out. So Jessie just went out on the edge of her little balcony and hung by her fingertips until she got up the courage to let go. It wasn't that far to drop, and there was only grass beneath her, but it looked like a long way down. The trick was to close your eyes and hold your breath for a second and then let go, and that is just what Jessie did.

She'd almost forgotten the cross that Mrs. Davis had given her and had to go back in to get it. Jessie had taken it off when she'd gone to bed, and put it on her bedside table. She'd remembered it just as she was about to drop from the balcony, and it had been a struggle to climb back up. She'd shoved the cross into the pocket of the dark windbreaker she'd put on and went back out on the balcony. Then she'd gone back inside again and got her cell phone from her purse, slipping it into the pocket of the windbreaker, too.

She eased silently through the hedges that bordered their back yard. She still had a key to Kira's car, and it was parked on the street in front of the Matthews' house, only a block away, right where Kira had always left it. She'd seen it yesterday and it had sent a pang right through her heart. Kira had loved that junky little car. She said a silent little prayer that no one would be awake at the Matthews' house, and that the car would start on the first try. And she sighed in relief when both of her little prayers came through.

She was on her way, but first she had a stop to make.

Just in case.

Father Raymond Sullivan didn't look very priest-like, at least the way that Jessie imagined priests were supposed to look. They should be tall and thin, with a grave ascetic face and always look calm and serene. Father Raymond didn't wear a white collar, and he abhorred black suits.

He tended to gravitate towards loud Hawaiian shirts and blue jeans. He was short and chubby, not tall and lean. And instead of piercing blue eyes, he had weak ones that tended to water all the time. He was nearsighted, and he wore big rimless glasses. And he poured sweat constantly and looked 'as nervous as a whore in church', as Mandy Hartwell had once described him. Her mother's religion had been a wishy-washy thing: sometimes she felt it, sometimes she didn't, but she told Jessie that she had made a promise to herself when she was pregnant with her that she would at least try to give her child a choice when it came to religion. And giving her a choice meant taking her to church at least once a month.

They'd tried out numerous churches before they'd settled on this one, and Jessie always had a suspicion that she'd chosen St. Anthony's because Father Raymond was the only minister she'd met who would argue with her. And Jessie allowed herself a little smile at the thought.

Mandy Hartwell had loved to argue, and she naturally distrusted those who would not defend their beliefs in the same way. Give way to her in misguided politeness long enough and she would view you in contempt. Reverend Snakeshit, she'd called one minister whose greasy smile and misogynistic hellfire and damnation sermon had annoyed her. The man had just blinked and stammered when confronted with her opinion of his views. Jessie had seen it happen time and time again; her mother simply did not like those who could not stand up to her.

And Father Raymond, for all he looked like a pushover, certainly could. He poured sweat and wiped his glasses furiously and doggedly defended his ideology when questioned. And in the process he'd earned a friend.

He might not look like a priest or act like a priest, Mandy had said admiringly of him. And I might think that half of what he believes is a crock of shit. But at least he knows how to shove back when I push him.

Jessie had never understood this playground concept of respect, but she knew it was the way that her mother thought, and she accepted it. She accepted it, because, like so many things about her mother, there was no changing it. She was the way she was. Father Raymond accepted it, too, and that made Jessie like him.

And Father Raymond did have one quality that priests needed. He knew how to be a good friend. When Jessie's mother had died, he'd been right there with her, and he didn't give her stupid platitudes or tell her she'd see her mother again one day. He'd simply sat with her on their lumpy old couch and cried with her, his arm around Jessie's shoulders. She could feel him shaking against her while she wept, and somehow that made her feel better, to know that someone else mourned as fiercely as she did.

And now he didn't ask Jessie stupid questions or act as if she needed to see a therapist when he found out what she wanted. He just gave her a small bottle of holy water without a second thought, as if many of his parishioners came after midnight with such a request.

"Father," Jessie asked quietly as she turned to leave. "Do you believe in pure evil?"

"I think that you can't attribute everything that happens in the world to God," he said. "I know that there are some who would not agree with me, but I think that there is evil in the world that God can't prevent or control." He took off his glasses and began to polish them on the corner of his bright blue and yellow patterned shirt. "And there is evil out there, Jessie," he said solemnly. "That is what is keeping me awake tonight. You be careful, you hear?"

And she promised that she would be.

* * *

The house that had been built where Abuela's old one used to stand was massive, three-storied, and it reminded Jessie of those old plantation houses that they'd had in the South before it fell to the Yankees. It had columns out front and a porch that extended around the house in a U shape. Because this was South Florida after all, the entire back of the house was a lanai, and the pool looked bigger than Olympic size.

Christ, it looks like Tara in Gone with the Wind, Jessie thought in disgust. Tara on steroids.

Pink bougainvillea cascaded everywhere, and there was bed after bed of dazzling flowers with colors so bright that they almost hurt the eyes, even in the dark.

But it seemed so out of place here, this plantation house and its beautiful gardens. It was stupid to go against nature. This monstrosity of a garden required ten times the water that the native plant life needed, and it would wither and die almost immediately if someone were to stop taking care of it. Because Jessie knew that if this house was left alone for just six months, the luxuriant gardens would be overgrown with vines and weeds. Palmetto bushes would creep forward. This was a sub-tropical land, and the plant life was unstoppable. It was fecund here, uncontrollable, and left to itself for just a short time, the land would claim back these gardens.

Jessie skirted the gardens and stepped into the undergrowth that bordered Abuela's old property. She smelled rotting plants and dank water underneath the canopy of scrub pines. Leaves rustled and something seemed to slip through the palmettos. Jessie slipped silently through, her anxiety rising. What if she'd remembered wrong? What if the house wasn't this way at all? Once, when something screeched horribly and flew past her face, Jessie thought that her heart would explode.

Then she saw that it was only of the little burrowing owls that were native to this area. Thirty years ago, the little owls that made their nests in the ground had been driven almost to extinction by the rush of construction, but they were now protected, and you weren't allowed to build within so many feet of their burrows. The owl preservation had been a big success, and their numbers had increased greatly. You saw the fierce little creatures all over the place, sitting on the wood poles that game wardens put up to mark their burrows. This one was no more than six inches tall, but he had made a noise big enough for ten owls and Jessie shook for ten minutes after their encounter.

And then she saw it.

The house.

It squatted there before her like some rancorous goblin, sucking all the light of the full moon from the sky and appearing to glow. Jessie drew nearer and went up the crumbling front steps to the front door, repulsed and yet drawn by the malignant shell of a house. The doorknob felt cold to her fingertips, just like it had in her dream.

She knew that they were waiting in there for her. He'd been calling her name. And she was going to stop him.

Jessie opened the door and went in.

It opened easily with no creaking, and she knew that someone had been to work on the old place. It made sense. They didn't want it to appear to be inhabited, but they didn't want the door to fall off when they pushed it, either. So they'd tightened and oiled the hinges, and done a little repair work that wouldn't show up unless you were looking for it.

The house was just as she remembered it, but now it was filled with old furniture, and of course there were those *charming* blood filled paintings on the walls. Jessie stared around. She was standing in the central room that they had found when they were children. Jessie shivered. She felt cold.

She knew from her dream and from her memory that there were two hallways that branched off from this room, and that one of them led only to a kitchen. She must go down the other hallway, the one that had frightened her so as a child. The hallway that led to the back of the house, and to what waited for her there. What she wanted was there. It was in one of the rooms there. She walked to the closest doorway and put her hand on the doorknob, trembling. The feel of the cold metal against her hand was real, but this all seemed so dream-like. She wasn't even sure that she believed in any of this, and yet here she was, alone, facing fears beyond her comprehension. But if none of it was real, that meant she was crazy. And she didn't feel crazy.

It was ridiculous, ridiculous that she was here, ridiculous to believe that there could even be such creatures as vampires and ghosts. Yet she was desperately praying that ghosts at least were real, because she didn't want to be alone, because she was horribly afraid that she couldn't do this by herself.

"Not all alone," said a familiar voice. ***"I'm here, baby. I came with you before, and I wouldn't desert you now."***

Jessie heard the voice with relief, because she had been on the verge of running. At least if she was crazy, she was crazy in a way that was helping her. Because Jessie knew that if she ran now, they would only come after her. Even if she escaped, they would get her, and who knew how many more would die.

It had to stop.

She forced herself to twist the doorknob. The sound of the door creaking open was hideously loud and unexpected, ripping and tearing at her already fragile nerves. Jessie found herself nearly in tears.

"Courage, baby," her Mom whispered in her ear. ***"Everybody's scared. Even the dead people."***

And Jessie had to giggle at that one a little bit.

"Funny, is it?" asked a voice, and Jessie saw a woman rise from the bed inside the room. She was dressed all in black, and her hair had been dyed a deep purple. She was about the same age as Jessie, maybe a little older. She wore black lipstick, and her fingernails were long and pointy, and painted black. She smiled, too, a smile that made her look sweet and lovely, and Jessie could see the way that she used to be. There was no real amusement in her expression now. The smile was malevolent and her eyes were wicked, and Jessie knew somehow that there was no humor left inside the girl anymore. Whatever had been there before was gone now, burned out by drugs and Sang Adorer.

"I guess it is funny, to you," the girl said, and Jessie saw that she was holding a gun.

She stood very still, waiting for the girl to fire and for this all to be done, knowing with a sick feeling down in her stomach that she had lost, that it was all over. The girl came toward her, and Jessie stared, tensed in every muscle. How had she gotten here? Had they made her a prisoner, was she hooked on drugs, did she just like this killing? What was her story?

When the girl was almost upon Jessie, something happened. A soft blanket of light seemed to envelop the girl, making her purple hair glow weirdly. She held the gun out to Jessie, a vacuous smile on her young face.

"Take the gun, Jessie," she said, but it wasn't her voice, it was Mom's. ***"Take it, 'cause you're gonna need it, later. This one is just going to sleep now."***

Jessie took the gun that the girl held out and watched in wonderment when she lay back down on the bed she had been reclining on when they entered. The girl seemed to fall instantly into sleep. Jessie stared, shaking, felt her hand cramp and realized that she still held the gun straight out before her, gripping it so tightly that it hurt. She loosed her grip and let the arm fall to her side. The gun felt cold and oily on her hand, and she shuddered.

"Jessie," whispered a voice from the center of the house. "Come and visit, come and visit me, Jessie."

She knew then that the girl had been a diversion, just a human shield for the real monster that lived in this house. She hadn't been valued at all, and if Jessie had killed her, it would only have been an amusement for him. He liked killing, even when others did it.

She stepped back into the hall, trying to see in every direction, refusing to allow panic to cloud her judgement. She would have to move quietly, even though Sang Adorer or whatever his name was knew that she was here. Because who knew what else was lurking in the dark waiting for her.

She moved along the hallway, a deep dread creeping up the back of her neck. She paused by a large spiral staircase, but saw nothing.

"Move, Jessie," Mom said. ***"It's above you."***

Jessie jumped out of the way, and a man landed lightly down in front of her, looking in his loose clothing like a huge black bat jumping down upon its prey. Where did he come from? Jessie thought. I swear he wasn't there when I looked before. She pointed the gun at him and he laughed.

"You can't kill me," he said and laughed uproariously. "I'm immortal. My master Sang Adorer has made me immortal."

Something made Jessie reach for the cross in her pocket, the one that Mrs. Davis had given her. She listened to her heart, the way that Grandma Belle had told her to. The man shrank back, hissing, when he saw it and Jessie knew what to do. She flung the cross at him with all her strength. It hit his neck and sank into the skin there like a knife into hot butter, and Jessie watched in horror as he fell and writhed upon the ground. The cross sank further and further beneath his skin, the chain slithering around his neck like a snake, until his head was severed from his body and rolled onto its side. Jessie cried out when the dead eyes seemed to look up at her, to accuse her. As she watched, his flesh wrinkled and withered and slowly became a large pile of dust.

She stared at the pile for a long time, fighting the urge to weep, or to scream out in hysterics. *I'm sorry*, she thought. *I'm sorry that you got involved in all of this, and I'm sorry that I'm responsible for your death.* She forced herself to pick up the cross out of the pile of dust and thrust it back into her pocket. She dropped the gun in with it. Somehow she knew that the gun would not help her now. She could hear the voice still calling her name. Calling her name and laughing. Laughing as if amused by the killing of its disciple.

She passed a room with an open door, and paused to look inside. Jessie saw a gallows-like platform with two steps up to it, perhaps two feet off of the ground, with a grate as the surface to stand on and a galvanized tub underneath. She knew then, sickly, that this was where they killed their victims and performed their blood rites.

"Come in," said two voices, and she realized that a young couple was huddled against the wall. They were both tall and blond and pale. They looked enough alike to be brother and sister, but Jessie hoped that they were not. The boy was stroking the girl's breast through the thin stuff of her black tee shirt, and she thrust her body lasciviously against his hand with a sigh of pleasure, gazing lovingly up at him.

"Come in and play," the boy said now, licking his lips. He'd never taken his eyes off of Jessie, even while his hand had been so busy with the girl. "Or we'll come out there and play."

And he started for her, the blond girl holding his hand. He reached one hand into the oversized pocket of his baggy jeans and pulled out a knife. He pushed a button on its side and the blade shot out, and Jessie was mesmerized by the glinting silver edge. She saw that the cutting edge still had rusty looking blood on it. He was grinning, and the girl was grinning, and Jessie knew that they would kill her, still smiling. And then they'd have sex right beside her cooling body, because that was what turned them on. She could see it, there, glinting in their eyes. She was frozen, and she knew that she was going to die.

And then her mother was there, Mandy Hartwell in all her glory, holding Jessie's hand. She pointed a finger at the two, and they seemed to see her as clearly as Jessie did, and they were horrified; the girl screamed out in terror when Jessie's mother took a step forward, still holding Jessie's hand.

"Go," Mom said, and her voice boomed just like it always had whenever she'd been angry about something. Jessie had seen her back grown men down with that booming voice and those flashing eyes. She would lift her chin, tighten her mouth and deepen her voice, and whoever it was that she faced would feel shamed, somehow, that they had not behaved. Even those who ordinarily had no conscience.

"It's been a bad dream, but now you're awake. Go to the police station and tell them what you've done. Turn yourself in. Perhaps it's not too late." She stared hard and resolutely at them, her eye grave and her face sad. ***"Because if you stay, you will die. I will kill you."***

The girl was whimpering now, holding on tightly to the boy's arm. And then they nearly trampled Jessie as they fled past her. She could hear their footsteps pounding down the hallway, and then she heard a door slam. Jessie looked wonderingly at Mom, who seemed to fade as she watched. And then Jessie was left clutching only air, because there was no hand in hers.

"I'm still with you," Mom's voice whispered inside Jessie's head. ***"I'm still here."***

Jessie walked on.

There were other doors, but she didn't open them. She wanted this to be over, and inside those doors would just be more diversions. The one she wanted was at the end of the hall.

She put her hand on the doorknob of the room at the end of the hall and hesitated. It was an old-fashioned door, like the rest of the house, and a key was sticking in the lock beneath the clear crystal doorknob. But Jessie knew that it wasn't locked. He wanted her to come in.

"I'm with you," Mind-Mom whispered. ***"I'm right here, too. You've got help. You're not alone."***

"I know," Jessie said out loud, and opened the door.

A fire was burning in the massive fireplace. In front of it stood the man who had come to her house. Jessie was struck again by his physical beauty. He was elegant in black silk, and the fire backlit his glorious silver gilt hair, adding rosy warmth to the cold paleness of his skin. His red, red lips curved into a slow, sensuous smile, but Jessie could see the rotten skull of her dream lying like a malignant shadow behind the beautiful face, and she was not charmed. And she could swear that there were figures in the fire behind him, demons and imps, burning and moaning, twisting and reaching out their fervent arms to try and touch him, to caress him with their heated limbs.

And Jessie finally admitted to herself that it was all real and not some hallucination; her mother, the ghost, was here with her in this room, and Sang Adorer was really a vampire. He was of the undead, and it was because of him that Shannon and Kira and Andy were dead. Because of him.

"Welcome," he said softly. "Welcome to my home. I welcome you here even though you turned me away so discourteously from your own home ... but no matter, you are here now. You're so smart, such a bright young woman. I called you and you came. You knew the way to me, but of course it was only because I was calling you."

"I've been here before," Jessie said stonily. "That's how I found this house. I've been here before, and it was easy to find it again. I didn't need your help, and I don't believe in your power. You're just some sick psychopath who's fried his brain with drugs."

Annoyance creased his perfect features, but he smiled. Jessie could see a red light flash in his eyes for a scant second and it frightened her.

"Perhaps," he said. He gestured around the room. "Come, join our party."

Jessie looked around with a start. She had been focused on him so intently that she hadn't looked around the room. There were people all around, all young, all dressed in black. They were all watching her with an avid expression that bordered on lust, and Jessie felt that she might faint. They were all his people; he had enslaved them just as he had enslaved the others she had met on the way to this room, and they did just what he wanted them to do. She knew that they could all converge on her at any second and tear her to pieces, just the way that they had done with all of their other victims.

She saw Dan Jackson among them, smiling eagerly at her and lounging indolently against a cushion in the corner. And she was never able to explain everything that happened after that, not to herself and not to anyone else.

Jessie was afraid, so very afraid; she dug down deep inside herself to try and banish the fear but the strength that unexpectedly came into her body did not come from the inside. It came from without, in a great overwhelming flood that somehow took her over. It was strong enough, this power, to stiffen her knees and keep her up on her feet. And Jessie felt that she was filled with a cold flame that would not be assuaged until it had vengeance. She pointed at Dan Jackson in sudden fury.

"Murderer!" she cried, and somehow it was Shannon's voice, not hers. "Murderer! You are just as responsible for all the deaths as this thing who calls itself your master."

Dan Jackson sat up, looking shaken.

Lifting her arms into the air, Jessie twirled, around and around, laughing. But it was not her voice that laughed, nor was it just one voice. It was hundreds upon thousands of voices, all laughing together, and it hurt the ears. Her audience watched with horror, even the demon Sang Adorer was afraid, and Jessie felt the power fill her up to the top with glorious light.

She could hear thoughts that were not her own, and the part of her mind that was still hers filled up to the brim with pity and horror.

(no oh no that hurts too much oh jesus it hurts have mercy mercy)

(help me help me Timmy's dead I saw him help me help me help me)

(momma momma momma)

And Jessie began to know things:

A woman ran through the snow on a frozen river, a woman with long black hair who had bare feet and was clothed only in a sleeveless nightdress. Her bare arms pumped at her sides, working for speed, and she looked behind her as she ran. Her cheeks were bright pink from her exertion; her nostrils opened wide as she panted and ran hard to get away from him. Her face was full of terror, and the monster who ran behind her laughed. He liked the terror that she felt; he fed off of it as surely as he would feed off of her blood. Sang Adorer leapt upon her and knocked her down. And the snow beside her was stained red with her blood.

A man dressed in a dark suit and blue shirt lay slumped on his back on the asphalt of a parking lot. One hand was raised above his head, the other crumpled beside him. His eyes were open wide and stared blindly up, because he would never see anything again. The overhead lights that surrounded the parking lot were reflected in his irises. There was a two-inch gash on the side of his throat, and a bright head bent over him and sucked eagerly at the blood that flowed down the side of his neck.

A woman clutched her two small children to her breast and begged for their lives. She offered herself instead, and Sang Adorer laughed and told her that young blood was the sweetest. And he made the mother watch while sank his fangs into the struggling, weeping children. And then he drank from her but she made no protest, simply lying there with no expression on her face as he sucked down her life. When he was done with them he cast them all aside like someone throwing away an empty beverage container.

And there were many, many more, and Jessie knew them all in the flash of an instant.

"You're all damned," she cried, and this time it was Andy's voice, deep and clear and strong. "You will all die and spend eternity in a pit of fire!"

The girl closest to her screamed, and pressed herself back away from Jessie, her hand over her mouth. The next voice that came from Jessie's mouth was achingly familiar to her, and she would weep later at the remembrance of it.

"I trusted you all, and so I died," Kira shouted. "But you won't go unpunished. You'll be punished now. My Jessie will punish you now."

And voices shrieking of vengeance poured from Jessie, as if she were merely the vessel to hold their angry souls. Her whole body shook with their passion and she strained to keep herself grounded, to not lose herself in the wash of their emotion.

"Steady," said her Mom, but the voice was not inside her head this time. It was right beside her and so was her mother. And on her other side, Jessie could vaguely make out the outline of a small ancient woman with skin like crumpled brown paper, a hooked nose and a coronet of dark braids. The three stood shoulder to shoulder in the room full of milling, violent strangers.

"The ones inside won't hurt you, and they won't let any harm come to you. Just stay calm and hold steady. Grandmother and I are here to help, too."

"Pay no attention to her," Sang Adorer cried to his disciples, and Jessie thought that he seemed smaller now. "It's only a trick."

"You know what to do. Do it now," her mother whispered. ***"Now, Jessie."***

Jessie pulled the vial of holy water that Father Raymond had given her from her pocket, uncorked it, and threw it at his face.

Sang Adorer shrieked and screamed, the sound wailing through the night. His hands flew to his face and Jessie could see the skin bubbling into huge blisters. He reeled in circles, one eye completely blinded, his flesh literally melting as the holy water boiled its way right through, and Jessie saw the bones of his face when he howled out to his followers in anger:

"Kill her, kill her!"

But his disciples were fleeing, trampling one another in their fury to be gone. They knocked each other down, they kicked and punched in their fury to be away from the voices of their victims. Jessie saw Dan Jackson crouched in a corner with his hands over his ears, sobbing.

And Jessie felt the power rise in her until it was near unbearable, until she felt that she would explode from the force of their rage. She pointed both her hands at the demon. A sound rose from her throat, a guttural sound of pain and fury, a howling of a million voices that rose into a cacophony. All who were near covered their ears. She could see the demon Sang Adorer shrieking and bending in upon himself, trying to get away from the noise that surrounded him.

She could feel a buzzing begin in her body, way down in her feet, and it sang its way joyously through her, growing stronger and stronger as it surged ever upward. She jerked with the force of it, with the *power.* When it reached the ends of her hands, she felt a whispering rush as the green swirling tide of light came flowing from her and hit Sang Adorer with the force of a hurricane. He screamed and writhed with the might of it, and he was immediately down upon the ground with his pain. And it seemed to Jessie as if she could hear hundreds upon thousands of voices inside that green light that flowered from her fingertips; and that the voices were all whispering their own name, over and over again, and that the voices she heard crying out were the voices of the ones that he had killed.

And that they had come to kill him.

It seemed to last forever, that green light/sound/cry. It went on and on and on, and when it finally stopped pulsing from her fingertips, Sang Adorer lay prone upon the floor.

Jessie's ears felt empty now that the voices were gone; she was hollow inside, and suddenly, achingly lonely. She would hear those voices in her dreams for years to come and she would always wake afterward with a smile on her face, gladdened by them. She had *known* them for those moments, she had *been* them all in some strange way, and she was always glad when they came to visit her in her dreams.

Jessie stared at Sang Adorer, his body seeming less substantial. It seemed to take up less space in a way that Jessie couldn't pinpoint. Then she realized in horror that he was fading, and while she watched, he disappeared from view. And she knew with a sick feeling down inside her stomach that it had not worked, not completely. They had only weakened him; he was not dead at all, but merely gone from this place.

She stared dully around her, at the few of his people who were still here, cowering in the corners, afraid. She pointed the gun at them. There was still something else that she needed.

"Tie him up," she said to one girl, gesturing with the gun at Dan Jackson. "I'll kill all of you if I have to, so don't even think about leaving."

But she needn't have worried, for they had all been cowed by the events of the night and they scurried to do her bidding. The weeping Dan Jackson was bound tightly and Jessie made two of them drag him out into the hallway. Then Jessie motioned them all to the back of the room.

"Stay here," she ordered. "Wait for the police to come. I know who you are, and I'll get you if you try to leave."

And they believed her, all of them. She locked them in the room. She hoped that they were still sufficiently frightened of her to stay put, because she wasn't even sure that she could take care of Dan, and he was tied like a steer for branding.

Once she was alone in the hallway, she pulled her cell phone from her pocket and called 911. She gave them concise directions to the house in a calm voice, then hung up. Then she called John Bennett, giving him the same directions in the same calm voice and hanging up again.

She had no time for their questions. She still had something to do.

"Talk to me, Dan," Jessie said. "I have to know some things. It's all over now, so what does it matter if I know? Tell me. Why'd you leave that package underneath your pillow for me to find? You had to know that somebody would come looking for you eventually, so why'd you put all that stuff underneath your pillow?"

"That wasn't me, that was Shannon," he said sharply. "Do I look that dumb to you? She couldn't take it when we started killing people that she knew. It was all right as long as it was strangers, but when we started killing her former friends... He was smart, you know. He was the one who found all of the people who knew how to cook up the meth, and he brought us to this house. It's way out away from everything; there aren't any close neighbors. So there was nobody around to smell it, 'cause it stinks really bad when you're cooking it, you know. And if we made a little noise, nobody heard. And we got a whole chain of distributors going, but I had a lot to do with that. We had money, lots of money; we made nearly enough to buy all of Florida, and that was because of me. Some of our little chain started taking way too much of their own product and went a little crazy. But overall, it was working out pretty good. Yeah, I'm just as smart as him," Dan boasted. "He was a vampire hiding inside a group of people who liked to pretend to be vampires. So he looked normal, you know? Until you got to realize that he was the real thing, not a fake."

"All right," Jessie said roughly. "Get over all the admiration for yourself and your freak boss and tell me about Shannon." When he began to act reluctant, she brandished the gun at him, and he began to talk again. Then the words poured from him, as if he had been dying to tell someone all that he knew.

"We met at a party, and I started feeding her drugs, right away, and then she met him. He hypnotized her, somehow, the first time she ever met him, and she would have done anything for him. He would call to her, and it didn't matter where she was or what time it was, she would come to him. She helped us distribute the meth that we were making, and she took a lot of it herself."

Dan grinned. "She might have acted all right around you, but she was the one of the worst of us for a while. Part of it was the money. She liked the money, but don't fool yourself, it wasn't only the money. Part of it was bloodlust, too. Man, she sure did like killing people . . . It started wearing off after we killed Kira. And then he made her start having sex with him, and with all of us . . . she started pulling away. She even tried to talk us out of killing Andy. She talked to me about you after Kira was killed, about how you wanted her to ask her friends all these questions. She begged me not to tell him, but of course I did. He was my master. I tried to calm her down, and I told her I'd scare you off without hurting you. I made that phone call, and I came to your house that night, but it didn't work." He shook his head at her in mock sorrow.

"You should have backed off, and she might be still alive." Dan laughed when Jessie flinched at his words, but he wiped the smile off of his face and began to talk again when she pointed the gun at him threateningly.

"After he came to see you, she freaked. Sang told me to stop going to work, and to move out to the house. He knew that she'd tell you something, eventually, and he didn't want to make it too easy for you. And he was right, wasn't he? She knew that I'd told him, and that if he'd gotten in that night, he'd have killed you and that little old lady you live with. And then she found out that he had given your name to some of the other people in the group and told them that you were our enemy. And the ones who had your name weren't acting so stable anymore, and that scared her even more. Like Sylvia, who shot at you. Shannon wanted you to find all that stuff, she wanted out, and she knew that you'd come there, to my apartment. So she left it for you to find. I almost got you that afternoon, you know. Sang told me that you were there, and you'd only been gone a couple of minutes when I arrived."

He laughed again, and Jessie's skin crawled when she remembered how her mother had warned her to get out of his apartment, and how she'd run down the street like a madwoman. Everything would have turned out so differently if she hadn't left when she did.

"She wanted to get caught and she knew that she would if you got the right information. She said you were stubborn, and she was afraid that you might hear something about this house. She said that you'd all been here before, when you were kids. So I wanted to kill you, but she begged me not to." Dan sneered. "She couldn't handle it. She said we'd become something evil, and that she wanted it to stop."

He grinned slowly, and Jessie had the crazy thought that if they'd met before he got mixed in with all this weirdness, she would have liked him. His next words put any thought of liking him right out of her head.

"I knew it was evil. I knew it, and I didn't care. I wanted it to be more depraved and immoral than it already was. I wanted to break every law known to God and man. I liked it."

"Why'd you do it, Dan? Why'd you kill all those people?" Jessie screamed at him in sudden anger. She aimed a kick at his leg, and then another when he didn't answer. She pulled back her leg for another kick, and he finally spoke.

"It was for Him. For the ceremony," Dan said sullenly. "We had to have them for the ceremony. We'd have them on Fridays, down at the house. Not every Friday, because we couldn't always find somebody to kill. I picked up some woman one night while she was waiting for the bus, but we couldn't count on that happening all that time. That was just my good luck. The next time, we just picked up some old bum from the street, and then we lucked onto a couple runaways. But hey, we didn't want to come down with AIDs or hepatitis or something. We had to have clean victims. And he liked them best when they were young, in their early twenties."

Jessie took a step back and leaned against the wall.

Some woman who was waiting for the bus.

She felt shaky, and her eyes burned the way they did when she was going to throw up. She slid down until she was sitting on the floor. Dan hadn't even noticed, just kept yakking away, all proud of his sick self, she thought with revulsion.

"So it was my idea to meet people online and get them to trust me. I was already working down at the Beach Bum, and I'd go online all the time, messing with people, so I thought it was a good way to find victims. As soon as we hooked up in person, I'd start feeding them crank and other stuff and getting them dependent on the drugs, and on me. Then I'd get them to come to a 'Goth' party with me. We all did it, after the first time worked so well. Even Shannon. There's probably been about ten or eleven of them so far. There'd have been more, but you know, it takes so long to work up a sacrifice. Took a long time to get some of them to trust us. What's the world coming to, I ask you."

Dan let out a high pitched cackle.

"You know, there's a lot of crazies out there. So people aren't as credulous as they should be." He giggled to himself for a while, straining at his bonds. He lifted up his head to glare at Jessie, the naked hate in his eyes a shock to her, even knowing what he was.

"I'd cut you up and drink your blood if I could. If I ever get loose, you better run and run, little girl."

"You're not getting loose," Jessie said. "Now tell me about the ceremony."

"We liked to get cranked up first. We cranked them up, too, so it'd seem like a bad dream to them at first. We always put it in a soda, because you can't taste it that way. There's just nothing like killing somebody when you're high. It's like a movie, like one of those teenage slasher flicks. All that blood and gore," he said dreamily. "I loved it. We'd always kill them on the platform and drain all the blood into a tub. There was gallons and gallons of it, and he'd drink his fill. Then afterwards we'd have a party and make cocktails from the blood that was left. Some people couldn't wait, and they'd be up there licking up all the blood and stuff off of the wood. I think he probably drank from them when we couldn't get a victim, though he always said he wouldn't, and that's why they were like that. He said we weren't sheep, we were wolves, and he couldn't drink the blood of his brothers and sisters. But I saw how he acted when he was hungry, and I was there the night he killed Shannon. He said it was because she'd betrayed him, but it was just because he needed blood. We're all his sheep when he needs blood. I know that he didn't just kill on Friday nights, either, 'cause he'd be all pumped and flushed and glowing sometimes when I'd see him, the way he always was after he drank. I think he's been at me, too, because I got to where I couldn't wait for it, either."

Dan grinned at her. "You're looking kinda green, Jessie." He laughed. "Want me to tell you how it was for your little friends, huh? How Andy begged and begged and I cut his throat anyway? How that Kira girl screamed for her mother through the whole ceremony and it got us so hot we slashed her to pieces, just kept slashing and slashing until there was hardly anything left of her, she was just a warm puddle of glorious blood."

Jessie's hand trembled on the gun. She balanced her arm on her knee and pointed it at him. She began to put pressure on the trigger. Why was he alive, and not Mom? How could this piece of dirt live and Kira and Andy be dead? He should die, too, not live in some prison growing fat.

"Don't do it, Jessie," Mind-Mom said loudly. ***"The best retaliation is to let this one live, can't you see that?"***

"What was that?" Dan said, trying to twist around. "Who else is here?"

"Your doom," Jessie said steadily, though her hands still shook. She eased the pressure off of the trigger, and put the hand holding the gun down on the floor. "The one person who could make me not kill you. You're terrified of jail, aren't you? You feel like you've been in jail all your life, living in this town, living with that old bat who has the nerve to call herself your grandmother. You can't stand walls, not real ones or ones in your head, can you? That's why you keep goading me. You want me to kill you. But it's not going to happen. You're going to be inside walls for the rest of your life. It's going to be worse for you, Dan, because you know what it's going to be like. Because it's the same way your whole life has been for the last ten years."

"Shut up, bitch," Dan shrieked, flailing around on the ground, but the knots were tied too tightly, and he couldn't reach her. "I'll get loose and I'll give you to him. He's not dead, you know. I would know if he were, because I'm part of him! I'll drink your blood, and then I'll smash your bones!"

"No, you won't," Mind-Mom whispered, her voice full of sorrow. Jessie could see her form between them, one slender arm reaching toward him but never touching. And it seemed as if Dan could see her too, because he howled out even more loudly and tried to crawl away, to back away from the lady who had tears on her face.

"Oh, you won't, Dan, you won't, you'll just lie in that narrow bed in some prison and dream at night about what a good life you could have had if things had been different. And it could have been, you know. You could have had a wonderful life, if only your mother had lived. You'll live in a waking nightmare. Poor boy, poor boy. She loved you, really loved you. But she won't come to you, Dan, **she** ***won't come to help you because you're evil, evil now, and her soul hurts for you. You killed me, Dan. I was just waiting for the bus, waiting to go home and***

be with my baby. You were still human that night, Dan, but you're not any more, because now you've given your spirit over to evil. You knew I had a daughter, I had told you so while we were sitting at the bus stop. You knew if you went through with it that you were leaving Jessie all alone, and you knew what that could do to a person because it had been done to you. You could have stopped it that night, Dan. Even after all the things that you done, you weren't an evil person, and you could have changed it all. You could have turned your back on the whole thing and become the person you were meant to be. Something in you told you not to do it, but you did it anyway. And now you don't even remember how many it was that you killed. You could have stopped it all, and your mother knows that. And so do you."

"Not true, not true!" he screamed. "Shut up, make her stop!" He screamed and screamed and screamed, and he couldn't see her anymore. But he could still hear her whispering it over and over.

"Poor boy, poor boy."

So he kept on screaming, until Bennett and the ambulance arrived and the EMT gave him a shot to sedate him. But Jessie crouched, crying, against the wall where she had leaned an eternity ago. She hadn't moved even when Bennett took the gun away from her. She could still see Dan's throat moving spasmodically as they loaded him into the ambulance. She could tell that in his mind he was still hearing the words her mother had spoken, and that he was still screaming.

* * *

"I'm going away for a little while, baby," Mom said in her sing-songy voice. ***"I'm going away, but I'll be back whenever you need me. You don't really need me any more."***

"I can dream you whenever I want to," Jessie said to her. "Isn't that what you are, a dream?"

"I'm whatever you want me to be," Mom said, and she stroked a strand of hair back from Jessie's forehead. ***"And you can dream whatever you want."***

"That's about the same kind of shit answer I used to get from you in real life," Jessie complained. "What in the hell is that supposed to mean?"

"I don't care if you are old enough to go to college, I can still whip your butt, girl," Mom said, that one eyebrow rising right up into her hairline. Girl came out like gur-rell, too, so Jessie knew she was pissed.

"Well, if this is my dream, I ought to be able to say what I want," she said stubbornly. "And I want you to stay."

"Business to take care of," Mom said breezily.

"What kind of business?" Jesse asked fretfully.

"I'm so sorry that you had to grow up so fast," Mom said. ***"I can't tell you how sorry I am that this all had to happen."***

"You can't fix everything, Mom," Jessie said, and watched a little smile play across her mother's wide, mobile mouth.

"Maybe I can," she said. ***"Maybe I'm the Magic Mom."***

"I haven't believed that since I was eight years old," Jessie said wryly, but she was lying. Somewhere in the depths of her mind, she thought that her Mom could do anything. Even come back from the dead.

"Maybe you believe in a lot of things that you say you don't," Mom said, just as if Jessie had spoken the words aloud. ***"Grandma Belle says to tell you that she's proud of you."*** Trailing her lips softly across Jessie's face, she turned and was gone.

The ringing phone woke Jessie from a sound sleep. Bennett had brought her to the hospital, and they'd decided to sedate her and keep her overnight, given the fact that she'd kept babbling about discovering her Mother's killer and ghosts and vampires and because she couldn't stop crying. Whatever it was that had been in that shot had worked because ten minutes after they had given it to her, she was laid out on the bed with a goofy smile on her face. Bennett had made Mrs. Davis go home and go to bed, because he said that Jessie would be okay, and he was right. Yeah, after that shot everything was all right. No more ghosts, no more tears, but maybe a benign hallucination or two. No wonder people turned into drug addicts if that was the way that it made you feel.

She'd woken a couple of times in the night to find a nurse sitting by her bed, probably courtesy of the cop who tried to pretend to be tough. She could barely focus her eyes even now.

"'Lo," she mumbled.

"Jess," Bennett said gruffly. "I just got off the phone with someone who says she's your Aunt Lucinda. Says she's in Paris and a few days ago she got a message she should call her sister. When she couldn't get in touch with her, she got worried. She finally got hold of your old landlady who told her what had happened. She says to tell you she'll be here day after tomorrow."

Jessie smiled groggily.

"You know anything about this, Jessie? Did you finally get in touch with your Aunt?"

"No," she said, laughing. It was no use trying to pretend anymore that it all had been a dream. It had all been real; the vampire, her mother, the strange power that she'd felt ... "But I bet I know who did."

EPILOGUE

This place was wonderful. He loved it here. He could not understand why he had never come here before. Look at all those who frolicked around him in these streets at night. There were endless opportunities for taking money from the unsuspecting. And there were so many, many opportunities for feeding.

This time he wouldn't make any mistakes. There would be no troubles as there had been all the times before. The last time he had overstepped his boundaries and grown careless because of his belief in himself and the power that he held. But not this time. He had learned something from the errors that he had made.

This time it would all be different.

Printed in the United States
1139500001BA/263

9 781591 133490